Pitch Please

There's No Crying in Baseball Series- Book 1

Lani Lynn Vale

Copyright © 2017 Lani Lynn Vale

All rights reserved.

**ISBN-13:
978-1975803612**

**ISBN-10:
1975803612**

Dedication

To my husband, who gave me an appreciation for baseball pants. Your butt will always look the finest, no matter how old we are. I love you!

Acknowledgements

Michael Stokes. BT Urruela. Y'all make a fine team! I love this picture!

CONTENTS

Chapter 1- Page 9
Chapter 2- Page 13
Chapter 3- Page 23
Chapter 4- Page 31
Chapter 5- Page 39
Chapter 6- Page 57
Chapter 7- Page 67
Chapter 8- Page 77
Chapter 9- Page 91
Chapter 10- Page 103
Chapter 11- Page 115
Chapter 12- Page 123
Chapter 13- Page 133
Chapter 14- Page 153
Chapter 15- Page 177
Chapter 16- Page 189
Chapter 17- Page 201
Chapter 18- Page 207
Chapter 19- Page 219
Chapter 20- Page 225
Chapter 21- Page 233
Chapter 22- Page 239
Chapter 23- Page 255
Chapter 24- Page 265
Chapter 25- Page 277
Epilogue- Page 285

Other titles by Lani Lynn Vale:

The Freebirds

Boomtown

Highway Don't Care

Another One Bites the Dust

Last Day of My Life

Texas Tornado

I Don't Dance

The Heroes of The Dixie Wardens MC

Lights To My Siren

Halligan To My Axe

Kevlar To My Vest

Keys To My Cuffs

Life To My Flight

Charge To My Line

Counter To My Intelligence

Right To My Wrong

Code 11- KPD SWAT

Center Mass

Double Tap

Bang Switch

Execution Style

Charlie Foxtrot

Pitch Please

Kill Shot

Coup De Grace

The Uncertain Saints

Whiskey Neat

Jack & Coke

Vodka On The Rocks

Bad Apple

Dirty Mother

Rusty Nail

The Kilgore Fire Series

Shock Advised

Flash Point

Oxygen Deprived

Controlled Burn

Put Out

I Like Big Dragons Series

I Like Big Dragons and I Cannot Lie

Dragons Need Love, Too

Oh, My Dragon

The Dixie Warden Rejects

Beard Mode

Fear the Beard

Son of a Beard

Lani Lynn Vale

I'm Only Here for the Beard

The Beard Made Me Do It

Beard Up

For the Love of Beard

There's No Crying in Baseball

Pitch Please

Hail Raisers

Hail No *(coming 9/27/17)*

Go to Hail *(coming 10/27/17)*

CHAPTER 1

Hockey gives me a zamboner.
-Text from Rainie to Sway

Hancock

Season opener at home
Texas Lumberjacks v. Michigan Marauders

"You're in my seat," I said to the beautiful woman. "Get up."

That beautiful woman, with her long brown hair and her nose stuck in the book she was currently reading, tilted her head up with a startled look that began to tug at my heartstrings before she even opened her pretty mouth.

I couldn't give in to it, though. She was in my seat. I *had* to sit there.

"I'm sorry," she whispered, grabbing her bag and scooting over like I'd grabbed her by her hair and physically yanked her out of my spot.

I hadn't done that, of course. Not that I wouldn't want to wrap my hand around her luscious, long locks and kiss the fuck out of her startled mouth.

"Parts," someone called.

I turned to find our starting pitcher, and my best friend, Gentry Green, staring at me like I'd grown a second head.

"What?" I snapped, wondering just what in the hell his problem was.

His mouth twitched, and I sighed.

"What?" I repeated, this time a little friendlier than the time before it.

The chick was fucking with my routine.

I was a superstitious guy. So, sue me.

I had to have my seat.

"I'm sorry," the woman whispered hastily as she resettled herself way away from her previous seat. "I didn't know it was taken."

"That one is taken, too," I muttered. "Brakes sits there."

She stood, this time upending her book onto the floor as she did.

I reached down and plucked it out of the spent sunflower seeds, handing it to her as I got a good look at the cover.

"You like baseball?" I asked teasingly, taking in the title of the book, *Baseball for Dummies*.

She blushed a harsh shade of red, and I immediately felt bad for teasing her.

The next minute, though, she yanked it out of my hand and turned to face forward, not looking back at me again.

Grinning like the shithead I was, I walked over to Gentry, AKA

Brakes, and held my hand out for the paint.

"That's number thirty-nine's sister." Gentry said. "The short stop on the other team."

"Really?" I asked in surprise. "Kid was a fuckin draft pick, right? Golden Glove."

Gentry nodded, and I swiped two stripes of paint. First under the right eye, second under the left.

Gentry took the paint and followed suit, only he did his left first, then the right.

It was always like that.

Baseball was a superstitious game. It was rare that we ever deviated from our routine.

"Why's she not their AT, then?" I asked.

Gentry shook his head and tossed the paint down into the stack of shit on the ground underneath his seat.

"Not a fucking clue. Girl's hot, though. I love that she's our athletic trainer."

I agreed with that. One hundred and sixty-nine percent.

She was thick and curvy, in all the right places, and I wanted to wrap my arms around her and kiss the hell out of her.

Crazy enough, I didn't think she'd be receptive to that.

Not yet, anyway.

She had on a Longview Lumberjacks team shirt, the tight khaki shorts that all the trainers wore, and a fucking ribbon in her hair.

She looked like my high school wet dream come true.

"You ready to warm up?" Gentry asked.

I nodded my head and started up the steps of the dugout, picking my bat up along the way.

I hefted it in my hands, tightening my grip around the wood, and breathed deeply.

"You first," Gentry nodded his head.

I walked ahead of him to the plate, nodding at the coach.

The coach nodded back, and I took my place at the plate.

Once I was there, I dropped the bat onto the plate so it rested against my thigh, put my gloves on, and pulled my pants up above my calves.

Routines.

All of it routine.

Once everything was perfectly in place, I fixed my hat, picked my bat up, tapped it six times on the plate, and lifted it to my shoulder.

CHAPTER 2

If you keep a baseball bat in your car, also be sure to keep a glove. Your lawyer will thank you.
-Word to the wise

Sway

Rainie (7:02 PM): This baseball game sucks. There's absolutely no cock sucking or pussy licking going on at all on third base.

I nearly choked when I read that message from my best friend.

Sway (7:02 PM): Why are you here again? And the game hasn't started, how do you know it sucks?

I looked up when I felt eyes on me, and nearly dropped my phone when I saw the bearded man who'd practically barked at me earlier staring me down. He'd just finished hitting, and I wasn't even aware he was back.

For such a big guy, he moved like a freakin' ninja.

His intense gray eyes, rimmed with beautifully long, dark eyelashes had me nearly choking on my tongue.

Why was he looking at me?

And oh, God. His beard was amazing.

Pairing that beard with those eyes, and the green hat pulled down low over his head—breathtaking.

That was before you even took in the rest of his body.

The man was covered in tattoos.

Not that you would be able to tell.

He didn't allow them to show for the first couple of games. As of right now, they were covered up with a long sleeved Under Armour compression shirt that fit him like a second skin.

Covering his tats was one of his superstitions—and it made me want to cry.

I loved his tattoos.

I wanted to lick every single one of them.

I had a Fathead sticker of him on my wall at home.

He was literally my favorite player on the Longview Lumberjacks, and would be in the entire league had my brother not played in the MLB as well. Though, it was a near toss-up.

I'd have a tough call today seeing as the Lumberjacks were playing his team

My brother was the short stop for the other team, and I loved him like crazy. But the Longview Lumberjacks–they were my team. Had been my team since I was old enough to sit in front of the TV with my dad and watch them play.

I think it'd broken my dad's heart a little bit when my brother had signed with the Sparks, but he was proud, nonetheless.

Parts took his hat off, readjusted it, and then put it back on. Five times.

Just like he always did.

I bit my lip and turned my head away, unable to look at that thick, dark hair and not orgasm.

It was beautiful, too.

I'd always had a thing for the tall, dark and dangerous look.

Bearded, tall, dark and dangerous…*well*…that was just my personal kryptonite.

My phone buzzed in my hands again, and I jumped.

Ember (7:22 PM): OMG! I can see you! Wave!

I looked up, startled, and glanced around. Then, for the second time, I dropped my goddamned book on the ground, exposing the stupid *Baseball for Dummies* to the world.

Again.

Sway (7:23 PM): Please tell me I didn't look as stupid as I felt.

Ember (7:23 PM): You look beautiful, stop whining.

I rolled my eyes.

Ember and I met at college where we were both studying to become athletic trainers. We met on the first day, and we instantly became friends.

We sort of grew apart for a while because we were going in different directions career wise—and, until recently, it had been a long time since we last spoke.

We picked right back up, as if we hadn't spent the last eight years apart. I was enjoying having her back in my life again.

Between her and Rainie, I was seriously loving life for the first time in years.

"Hey, anyone seen my fucking bubble gum?" a player yelled. "It was right here, and now it's gone. Oh, dammit, I'm missing two pieces. I only have five!"

I looked around for the lost candy, and idly wondered what the big deal was. If he had five, then that surely was enough to get him through the game, right?

Wrong.

Oh, how wrong I was.

"Hey," the player that I was having a very hard time ignoring interrupted my inner musings.

I turned, this time surprised that I couldn't see his eyes anymore.

He had on wraparound sunglasses that were tinted an intense shade of blue, and I liked them. A lot.

"Y-yes?" I stuttered.

"Can you go to the concession stand and get Manny a couple of Double Bubbles?" he asked.

I blinked, surprised that he would ask me.

"No," I immediately disagreed. "I'm the trainer. I can't just leave. What if someone gets hurt?"

His eyes stared at me steadily. "Because if he doesn't have all of his gum, he might be hurt. You don't want to be the cause of that, do you?"

I stared at him as if he'd grown seven heads that were all leaking snot.

"You're serious."

"Deadly."

I gave him a disbelieving look.

"I'm not leaving, but I'll ask my friend to get it for me. She's in the seats above the dugout," I explained when he gave me a dubious look. "You might be in luck."

He looked at me approvingly.

"I like your ingenuity," he grinned. "Is Bobby not coming back as head AT?"

I shook my head. "Bob had a heart attack about a month ago," I frowned. "He's okay, but he's had to slow down quite a bit. He might be back in an advisory capacity once he's fully healed; but, until then, I'm your man."

He chuckled, and I felt that dark, deep rumble in my soul.

"I like you, Half-Pint," he grinned. "I…"

I stiffened at the use of Half-Pint.

I was *not* a half pint.

I was a full pint. Maybe even a quart.

And I liked it.

Well, I didn't like it as much as I owned it.

I was curvy, and I knew it. I worked my ass off, ate the right shit, and I was still heavy.

It wasn't ever going to be different, and I accepted that, but the man didn't have to point it out to me or make fun of me by using demeaning nicknames.

But before I could snap at him, a coach yelled from the front of the dugout.

"Parts! You're up!"

Parts got up, leaving me with nothing else to do but text Rainie and ask her for two pieces of Double fucking Bubble.

Sway (7:30): Will you go buy me two pieces of Double Bubble? One of the players needs it.

"Did anyone find my gum yet?" Manny, number 11, called out. "Seriously, guys. One of you motherfuckers better not have eaten it."

Nobody answered, and I chose to ignore him as well.

My eyes staying on Hancock "Parts" Peters. Number 49.

He did his whole ritual.

Once he was there, he dropped the bat onto the plate, put his gloves on, and started his routine as he pulled his pants up above his calves, continuing on to adjust his hat and tap the plate with his bat.

Did he pull them down each time he was done hitting?

The thought made me smile as I watched the pitches start flying.

The first two were balls. The second two Hancock fouled.

The next one went straight at Hancock's head, and he dropped to the ground to avoid being hit.

Hancock got up, dusted himself off, and glared at the little fucker who'd nearly hit him.

And I do mean glare.

If there was a definition of glare in the dictionary, the look Hancock just sent the pitcher would be directly under it for emphasis.

He bent down and picked up his glasses that were laying in the dirt next to home plate, blew them off, then resituated them on his face.

Then he did his whole routine again with his bat, gloves, and pants. Followed by the hat adjustment, bat tapping and swinging it up to his shoulder.

Once when he was ready, he took his bat and aimed it high over the fence, indicating he was about to hit it over the fence.

My mouth dropped open at his audacity.

"Damn showoff," the coach muttered.

I hid my smile as I continued to watch.

The pitcher, Ramirez, sneered, and I knew what he was about to do.

He was going to hit him.

Knew it without a shadow of a doubt.

Ramirez reared back, lifted his leg and let the ball fly.

Hancock turned into the pitch, letting the ball smack into his right shoulder, and I groaned along with the entire stadium.

Ramirez had the fastest arm in the league right now, and being hit with a ball at ninety-eight miles an hour was enough to hurt anyone, even a big man like Hancock.

I stood up and was on the top steps of the dugout before Hancock even turned, and what I saw on his face was enough to send me back to my seat.

He wasn't hurt.

Or, at least, he wasn't going to show it.

He was, however, *pissed*.

Ramirez made it two more pitches, hitting one more player, before he was removed and replaced in only the first inning, and I found myself smiling.

Hancock, however, wasn't smiling when he was stranded on second and had to come in.

He started jogging to the dugout just as my phone chimed.

Rainie (7:51): Heads up!

I stood up and hurried to the steps, smiling happily when my friend tossed me a whole handful of Double Bubble.

"Thank you!" I called to her.

My gorgeous blonde best friend grinned at me and waved. I waved back and froze when her eyes widened and focused at something over my shoulder.

I turned slowly to find Hancock directly behind me, staring at me like I was an alien who'd invaded earth.

"What?" I snapped at him.

What was his deal?

"Throw those other ten pieces back at her, and only give Manny two." He looked at my hand. "He'll wig out even worse if you show up with that many."

I rolled my eyes and pocketed all but two pieces, then turned and headed back down the steps of the dugout.

Maybe, next game, I'd take the other trainers up on their offer to stay in the mouth of the tunnel entrance that headed out onto the field. Being in the dugout was turning out to be not such a good idea.

Especially when Hancock's next words hit me.

"I like the way your hips sway, Mizz AT."

I turned and narrowed my eyes at him.

"I don't like it when you mention my fat ass all the time," I growled. "And the name is Sway."

His eyebrows snapped together.

"I never once called you a fat ass," he sounded offended. "Not fucking once."

My lip curled. "Then why the nickname of 'Half-Pint' and saying you like the way my hips sway?"

"Because they do. And I fucking like it. There's nothing else to it but that," he said, taking a step back.

Then without another word he strapped on his catcher's gear, grabbed his glove and headed for the plate.

I watched him go, something uneasy settling in my chest.

"See you in three, Half-Pint."

Then he was gone, and I was left feeling unsure of what, exactly, had just transpired.

CHAPTER 3

Sleeping is too hard during the summer. Blankets are too warm, but without blankets I'm vulnerable to monsters.
-Sway's secret thoughts

Sway

I arrived at the stadium on time, and immediately headed down to the field.

The team, as well as all team personnel, were to be here on the field at one p.m. on the dot to film a freakin' commercial for ESPN.

I'd just stopped about halfway down the stairs that would lead me out onto the field when I looked up and spotted Hancock.

Parts.

What the hell did he want to be called?

Personally, 'Parts' was kind of hard to call someone. Which was why I started referring to him as Hancock in my mind.

Nobody called him Hancock, though.

Not the coaches. Not the news reporters. Not his teammates.

When he was addressed, he was Parts or Peters, his last name.

I felt particularly naughty addressing him as Hancock in my mind.

"Well, hello there, Half-Pint," Hancock drawled from the bottom of the stairs he was moving up. "What's going on?"

I smiled at him.

"We're to be here for a commercial, aren't we?" I asked, trying not to sound out of breath from the trek from my car to the stairs.

I was hopeful that they didn't actually want me to be here.

I was already incredibly uncomfortable in what they asked me to wear.

It was April, in the middle of fucking Texas.

With the owners requiring us to wear jeans, I was already sweating my ass off, and I'd only made a small hike from the car to the air-conditioned building.

It was enough to make me a sweaty mess, and I hadn't even made it to the eventful part of my day.

"Yes, we are," he agreed. "Well, you are. *I'm* not."

"Mr. Peters!" someone called from further down the stairs that led to the field. "Mr. Peters! Wait!"

Hancock looked over his shoulder, agitation clearly written all over his face.

"I've already told you I won't be doing it," Hancock informed the small man.

And he was small.

Maybe not compared to a normal man; but standing next to Hancock, the man looked positively minimal.

"Please," the man continued as if Hancock hadn't even spoken. "We've spent tens of thousands of dollars and months planning this commercial. Surely, you understand that we're doing it for…"

"Craig," Hancock growled. "I am not doing the Harlem Shake. Do I look like the kind of man who does the fucking Harlem Shake?"

Craig, who I guessed was the head of PR, smiled soothingly.

"Parts," he held out his hands placatingly.

I wondered again why he was called Parts, but I wasn't ever going to ask him.

It was weird, and it was also a big freakin' secret. Everyone in the entire league wondered and speculated about why he was called Parts. Nobody knew the story behind his nickname, though.

"I'll be there. But only if I can sit in the back and nobody sees me," Hancock conceded. "And don't try to move me, or I'm leaving. *Capisce?*"

Craig nodded his head urgently.

"How much time do we have until we start?" Hancock continued to question Craig.

"Oh, about twenty minutes or so. Do you need me to bring you anything to drink?" Craig looked hopeful, happy now that he'd gotten his way.

But I knew that Craig *hadn't* gotten his way.

Far from it.

If I had my guess, Hancock wouldn't even be in the commercial.

He'd literally stay on the sidelines and make it a point to stay out of every shot, just like he did after games when reporters were hoping to interview him.

Then there were the photos that featured him in them.

None of them were taken with his permission.

Other than his official team portrait, the one that the MLB used to show his stats during games, I'd never seen one picture of him looking at the camera.

"No, no drink, Craig. Thank you," Hancock waved Craig off.

The moment Craig was dismissed, he hurried back in the direction of the field, a freakin' skip in his step.

When he rounded the corner, I turned to face Hancock fully again.

"What?" I asked, wondering what that look on his face was about.

"I'm not doing the Harlem Shake," he repeated.

I held up my hands in understanding.

"I'm not much of a dancer, either. You and me can hang out in the back like the losers we are," I teased.

I hadn't meant that either of us were necessarily real losers or anything, and the moment the words left my lips, I realized how it sounded.

"I'm sorry," I said, holding up my hand. "In no way, shape, or form am I accusing you of being a loser."

He grinned.

"It's okay," he winked. "I don't dance. I don't do pictures. In fact, if I had my way, I wouldn't even be here right now."

I smiled shyly at him.

"Sway!" someone called. "Let's go! We have to sit together in the front."

Sinclair, the one man in the entire complex who I didn't want to see, was standing there sneering at me.

"She's not sitting in the front, Sinclair. She's sitting with me in the back. We have to talk about what I expect out of her this season," Hancock rumbled, stopping me with a large hand on my arm when I went to move around him.

Sinclair's face twisted in annoyance.

He wasn't my biggest fan.

I'd beaten him out for the job as head athletic trainer for the Lumberjacks, and he was, technically, my assistant when it came down to it. Needless to say, he was most unhappy about it, too.

"That's just the memo I got from the management team," Sinclair said sweetly. "I'm assuming it's okay that she sits with you, but you may want to make sure it's okay before she gets in trouble. I would hate for her to lose her job."

With that parting comment, Sinclair disappeared out onto the field, and I was left walking after him.

"Where are you going?" Hancock asked, latching on to my arm once again.

I tried to pull away, my heart starting to pound due to the amount of touching me he was doing today.

"If I don't go sit with him, he's going to try to make it seem like it was my fault that I wasn't sitting with them and probably over here screwing your brains out. He's been trying to get me fired since I got this job. I wouldn't put it past him to try to start a rumor about me seeing one of the players under my care."

His brows rose.

"He's that vindictive?" Hancock asked.

I nodded my head.

"I worked my ass off for this position. I'm not screwing it up because I don't want to be on national television."

He watched me walk away.

I could feel his gaze burning a hole into my back the entire way.

And he sat in the back for the entire commercial, too, not even tapping his foot to the beat.

Me? I probably looked ridiculous, but if I had to dance like a jackass to keep my job, then I'd do it.

Every freakin' day of the week.

***

Game 2 - later that evening

"This is like that time when Nolan Ryan hit Ventura with a pitch, and he stormed the mound only to have the snot beat out of him by an old man," I gasped in awe.

The man next to me, Jessup Steel, snorted.

"This is what they call the pissed off grizzly bear in him coming out," Jessup Steel was on his feet now.

All of us were. The entire team. The coaches. The other athletic trainers.

They were all waiting to see the outcome of the altercation.

The only thing holding the men in the dugout, at this point, was the coach and the assistant coaches.

"Have you seen my batting gloves? I had them, and then…oh, shit!"

The moment the first fist flew, the entire team, including the coaches, were out of the dugout.

I stood up, ready to do whatever I needed to do as well, but managed to stay on the top step of the dugout while the fight erupted.

I, however, wasn't stupid enough to get in between the flying fists and men.

I was a woman. A woman who'd never been in a fight in her life.

I wasn't shitting anyone. I was soft, and everybody knew it.

I wouldn't be able to stand up to the punches that were flying, whether I wanted to or not.

"You staying?" Sinclair sneered at me.

"Yep," I agreed.

"Stupid cunt."

Then he was gone, leaving me staring after him with hatred in my eyes.

CHAPTER 4

There's nothing like a largemouth on my rod.
-Fishing t-shirt

Hancock

So, I wasn't the most stable of men in the world.

Call me a hothead. I didn't give a fuck.

You fuck with my pitcher. You fuck with me. Simple as that.

"Watch your face when he comes after me," Gentry laughed. "Seriously, just look at it."

I did.

Gentry threw the first pitch, and nearly hit Crouse.

Crouse ducks, tosses Gentry a glare, and then readies for the next pitch.

Gentry, obviously not in the fucking around mood tonight, throws the pitch again.

And hits him.

Like he'd been intending to do the first time.

Not that we'd ever admit to that.

But Crouse was a fucking douchebag.

He never let you forget that he thought he was the superior catcher, even when he wasn't.

That, of course, was a good trait to have. *At times.*

When you were at bat, and talking shit to the other team's catcher, wasn't one of those times.

Before Crouse could even make it to Gentry, though, I was tackling him from behind.

The other man on second base, Diaz, headed for Gentry. Something that I hadn't seen at the time, due to the fact that I was busy beating the shit out of Crouse.

Diaz came at Gentry like a fucking battering ram, but Gentry caught him with a hooked arm around his neck, brought him down into a headlock, and proceeded to beat the shit out of him in return.

I'd just gotten Crouse on the ground underneath me when I got slammed from behind, my breath leaving me in whoosh.

It took ten minutes for the field to be fully cleared.

***

"Yo," someone snapped.

Sinclair, the other trainer who I didn't like, came up to me and started to touch me.

I immediately shook my head at him.

"Where's Sway? I asked. "You need to go check on second string."

Sinclair's jaw worked.

"Sway is currently being reprimanded," Sinclair's grin wasn't obvious, but I could read into his words.

"For what?" I barked.

"For entering the fight," he replied jovially. "You sure you don't need me?"

A shake of my head had him moving to the other men across the room, and I turned to glare at Gentry.

"She didn't enter that fight," I told him.

"How do you know?" he asked, leaning back in his ice bath.

I stood up and grabbed the towel next to my ice bath, and stepped out.

Once it was around my hips, I went in search of Sway, finding her in the coach's office.

"I didn't enter the fight, Coach," she was saying as I walked up. "I was in the dugout the entire time."

"That wasn't what Sinclair informed me," Coach Siggy replied. "I know you're protective of the boys, but we can't have personnel entering the fight, when we need them to set us straight after."

Coach Siggy was sporting his own shiner, and I wanted to laugh at the irony of the situation.

"She was in the dugout the entire time," I told coach. "Sinclair was mistaken."

"And how would you know?" Coach asked me.

I held up my bandaged arm.

"She wrapped this for me," I told him. "When I went looking for her, I found her biting her fingernails in the mouth of the dugout."

Coach Siggy sighed.

"You know I can't give you any special treatment here, darlin'." he said to her. "Keep your head up and your nose clean."

Sway smiled at Coach Siggy, and a rare smile crossed his face before disappearing again.

"How's my brother doing?" he asked.

Sway grinned.

"The last I checked in, he was winning his fantasy league and was extremely excited about it," she explained.

Coach snorted.

"Get out of here, girl. I'm sure you have a room full of men to take care of right now," he pointed to the door.

That's when Sway finally looked at me, and her eyes bugged out.

"Yes, Uncle Siggy," she whispered.

When she went to move past me, I turned to the side and barely stifled a groan when she passed.

Her sweet, tempting ass passed over my crotch so deliciously that I nearly moaned in delight.

It took everything I had not to grab a hold of her supple flesh and bend her over the coach's desk.

And now that I knew they were related, it might not be such a good idea to follow through with those thoughts.

"'Scuse me," she muttered, tossing me an apologetic look.

I gritted my teeth, and her eyes went down to my cock, which a second ago hadn't been nearly as hard as it was right now.

"You're excused," I lied through my teeth.

She smiled timidly, then raced off, her delicious breasts bouncing as she went.

Sweet Jesus. The way her ass swayed with each step had my mouth salivating.

When she was no longer in sight, I turned back to the coach to have him staring at me accusingly.

"Keep yours paws off my niece," he growled at me.

I held my hands up in the air.

"I would never."

He looked at my hands, moved to my face, and then went further down to the towel.

"Sure you wouldn't," he grumbled. "Get the fuck out."

Needless to say, I got the fuck out.

Then went straight to a certain someone.

I had a few aches and pains that needed to be seen to.

***

I laid down flat on the bench and stretched my legs out in front of me.

My head rested on the flat padded pillow while my feet hung off the bottom.

"What can I do for you today, Mr. Peters?" Sway's gentle voice cut into my thoughts.

I opened my eyes and nearly groaned.

Today she was wearing her jersey.

Usually, by this time in my evening, I was about two beers in, staring out over the lake with my feet kicked up on the balcony.

I lived off of Caddo Lake. My house was right off the water.

In fact, I was about as far out into the lake as I could be without having an actual houseboat.

Why I was here instead of at my place was beyond me, but I was here. I was horny. And I wanted Sway to come home with me.

Which might be the reason I was here acting like I was hurt and not at home with my beer.

"My leg feels like it's being stabbed," I pointed to my thigh where I'd caught a knee just below my groin.

She frowned and looked at it.

"Does it throb, or is it more of a constant sharp pain?" she asked. "Do you mind if I touch you?"

I shook my head, indicating my leg with my nod. "Feel free to touch all you want," I murmured. "As for the pain, it's more of a sharp pain."

My dick, however, *was* throbbing.

Thank fuck for my compression shorts I had on underneath my knit shorts that I'd changed into once I'd left coach's office.

"Did the ice bath help?" she questioned, placing her hand on my thigh.

My gut clenched in reaction to her hand being on my body, even if two articles of my clothing separated us.

"It did," I nodded my head. "But now that I'm not in there anymore, it's aching a lot more."

I wasn't talking about my leg at this point.

No, we were in dick territory now, and I wasn't quite sure how to extricate myself from the situation I found myself in.

I was already covering up my dick with my hand.

There was absolutely no way that she would miss it if I stood up.

"Show me where it hurts," she held out her hand for me to take.

Coach's niece. Coach's niece. Coach's niece.

I chanted the words as she felt me up.

I reluctantly took her hand, and I had to clear my throat to cover the groan at the feel of her hand in mine.

It was so soft, and it would feel perfect wrapped around my cock.

"Listen," I started to sit up. "I forgot I had to tell Coach something…"

She rolled her eyes and pushed me back down when I went to sit up.

"You're not moving until I inspect this sore spot."

And she did just that.

Twenty minutes and a fucking massage on the inside of my thigh later, and I was practically sprinting to my truck.

CHAPTER 5

I speak fluent baseball.
-T-shirt

Sway

Screamer hit deep, Wang Hurt

I blinked at the headline.

"They did not write that in the paper," I mumbled to myself, staring at the paper like something off of Punk'd.

"What are you mumbling about?" Ember asked from the seat beside me.

I tossed the paper into her lap, and she looked down.

It took her about fifteen seconds before she burst out laughing.

"Wang really is hurt," I informed her. "He pulled a hamstring, and I expect him to be out for about five games."

Ember looked over at me, a huge smile on her face.

"So, tell me more about Parts," she ordered. "You told me that he was nice. Is that true?"

I thought about that for a moment. He was nice—to me.

He wasn't nice to anyone else, though.

Not even other women.

"He's nice to me," I gave her. "But I'm not sure if that's because he wants to get into my pants, or because he actually likes me."

Ember grinned.

"He's one of my favorites," she smiled. "Did you know his brother, his twin, is a military contractor? That he used to be in the Air Force?"

My brows went up.

"No, I did not. How did you figure that out?" I asked suspiciously.

I knew everything there was to know about Hancock.

He was my favorite player in the league and I read every single article about him that came out. Surely, if his brother was in the military, that would be something flagged front and center in the news.

"His brother is friends with my husband," she smiled. "He's proud of Hancock."

Now *that* didn't surprise me. I was proud of Hancock, too. He'd come a long way in the six years he'd been playing professional baseball.

When he'd first entered the major leagues from the minors, it had been with a Texas-sized chip on his shoulder and something to prove.

It'd taken him three games to prove it, and he'd gone from the backup catcher to the starting catcher in that short amount of time.

Unfortunately, it was his inability to control his temper when it came to trash-talking the opposing team's players that made it difficult for him to hang on to the position.

Until suddenly, one day, he wasn't acting on his temper anymore.

That wasn't to say that he still didn't get into fights every once in a while. But that was completely normal for any player.

Then there was Crouse, the catcher for the Las Vegas Vikings.

He was the one man who could get under Hancock's skin every single time they played, and this game was just the beginning of the series.

"I'm sure Hancock is pretty proud of his brother," I offered.

"I am."

My belly flipped, and I turned to look over my left shoulder.

"Uhhh," I hesitated, finding Hancock standing there in jeans and a white t-shirt.

Hancock grinned. "I don't mind that you know about my brother, but I'd appreciate it if you kept it to yourself. We try to keep the fact that I'm hot shit private so the bad guys don't think to use him for ransom in case he gets captured or something."

My mouth dropped open.

"You're serious?" I asked in alarm.

He nodded his head.

Then a thought occurred to me.

"Is that why you don't take pictures?" I whispered.

Except the whisper came out just as loud as my normal voice, causing Hancock, as well as Ember, to start laughing at me.

"No," he shook his head. "I don't like pictures because I don't like pictures."

"Oh," I leaned back in my chair, then suddenly jumped up. "Are you okay?"

He held up his hand.

"Sit back down," he ordered me.

I narrowed my eyes.

"I'm not hurt. Nor do I need your services."

Ember snickered at my side, and I shot a glare in her direction.

She held her hands up in acquiescence. "Sorry, sorry."

Hancock's eyes went to her.

"And you are?" he drawled.

I was just about to retake my seat when I jumped back up, grabbing a hold of Hancock's hand and dragging him to stand in front of Ember.

"Ember," I dropped his hand. "This is Hancock Peters. Hancock, this is my good friend, Ember. She and I attended college together."

Hancock offered his hand, and I had the irrational urge to slap Ember's hand away, even though she was married to a very sexy exotic-looking man named Gabe. *Happily married with two kids.*

Get control of yourself, Sway!

Ember took his hand for only the barest of seconds, and then looked back at me.

"I've heard a lot about you over the last couple of weeks," she smiled. "You know you're Sway's fav…"

I interrupted my good friend before she could decide to spill the beans. It wouldn't do to give the man a bigger head than he already had.

"Then why are you in my office, Hancock?" I blurted.

He looked from me to Ember, and then back to me, before he smiled and shook his head.

"Nothing," he mumbled. "Just wanted to see if you'd go to breakfast with me."

"I'm leaving!" Ember exclaimed quickly.

Too quickly.

It was more than obvious that she hadn't originally planned on leaving.

In fact, she'd stopped to get donuts to bring with her.

Donuts that I was trying really, really hard not to shove into my mouth.

Hancock's gaze went to the untouched donuts on my desk, then moved to Ember. He grinned widely.

"You said your husband knows my brother?" he asked.

She nodded emphatically.

"He does."

If I didn't know better, I would say that Ember was a little starstruck.

"I'd love to meet him some time. Does he come to games?" he asked.

Ember's eyes widened. "Every once in a while."

He smiled. "I'll drop two tickets at the gate for you. I'd love to meet him."

Ember started to nod somewhat frantically.

"I think he'd like that," she gushed.

I rolled my eyes, and nearly laughed when she rushed to gather her things.

"I'll see you tonight for the party?" Ember asked hopefully.

I looked over at Hancock, then back to Ember.

"Yeah," I agreed. "I'll be there once the game is over."

Ember was backing out of the room when she suddenly stopped.

"If you'd like to bring Hancock, that'd be super," she whispered to me just before she left the room completely. "Good luck tonight!"

***

Once we arrived at Waffle House of all places, Hancock went back to the interrogation.

"Your brother's a baseball player, right?" Hancock asked, his eyebrows lifting with his question.

I nodded my head.

"He is," I confirmed, wondering where he was going with this. "For the Sparks."

"Then him being in the Major Leagues has to mean that he didn't just start being a baseball player last week," he continued.

I shook my head.

"No, he's been playing since he was six and I was five," I explained. "Why?"

His mouth kicked up at one corner.

"You reading *Baseball for Dummies*?" he hinted. "You've seen your brother play."

I promptly blushed.

"My best friend, Rainie, was responsible for that," I muttered, lifting my coffee cup to my mouth and taking a sip. "She thought she'd be funny and give it to me on my first big day right before the game. I opened it in the dugout."

"Ahhh," he nodded his head. "The blonde?"

I grinned.

"You saw her?" I guessed.

"It's kind of hard *not* to see her," he admitted.

I started to laugh.

"Rainie is an all-in kind of girl. She doesn't do anything halfway if she can manage all the way," I told him.

Explaining anything about Rainie was difficult to do at the best of times. Explaining her to a man like Hancock seemed rather impossible.

Hancock's lips twitched as he tried to keep himself from laughing.

"What does your Rainie do?" he asked, leaning back so his legs could stretch out in front of him.

The movement put his legs directly against mine, and I struggled with not yanking my legs back as far as I could make them go.

Surely, it would be okay to allow his legs to touch mine…right?

"Rainie is a free spirit," I told him, fondness for my best friend leeching into my voice. "She's had eight jobs in the last two months, and she's lived in three different apartments."

"How does she manage to do that?" he asked curiously.

I took another sip of my coffee before answering.

"Her daddy is a bad ass lawyer who funds all of Rainie's crazy whims," I disclosed. "He pays her rent. Pays for her car. Pays for anything and everything. Pretty much allows Rainie to do whatever the hell she wants to do."

Hancock lost his fight with his smile.

"Must be nice," he muttered, taking his own sip of coffee.

My brows rose at that.

"Last I heard, you had a multi-million-dollar contract under way with the Lumberjacks," I murmured. "Seems to me like you're not hurting for money."

Hancock nodded.

"I'm not," he agreed. "Anymore," he added. "But when I was younger…" he shook his head. "We survived on Ramen noodles, Beanie Weenies and peanut butter. And those were our good days."

"Hmm," I murmured. "We didn't eat anything we didn't grow or kill ourselves," I informed him. "I think I was a senior in high school before we ate out for the first time."

Hancock's foot twitched, and I had to hold my breath when his bare foot touched mine.

We were both in flip-flops due to the excessive Texas heat, and that meant that we were skin on skin when he touched me underneath the table.

He watched me squirm with a gleam in his eyes, and I was just about to pull away when he stopped, his foot next to mine, and asked me his next question.

"What have you been doing since you graduated?" he asked. "Was this always a place you wanted to work for?"

I nodded my head.

"I wanted to work for the Sparks, actually, but then my brother got signed there, and I decided that I couldn't handle seeing him every day. So, I applied here," I grinned. "I'd been interning for Bob for a while when I was free, so it was nice to step right in as head athletic trainer when he decided to retire due to his heart attack."

"Baseball season is long," he agreed. "And Bob was old as fuck. It doesn't surprise me that he signed on the dotted line."

"So, in short, I really do know my shit when it comes to baseball," I smiled. "I was head athletic trainer at UT Tyler for a couple of years before I got this job. A job I didn't think I'd get," I pointed out.

He set his empty coffee cup on the table in front of us and looked at me with those intriguing gray eyes.

Was it normal for eyes to be such an intense shade of gray?

And, oh my God. He had powdered sugar in his beard from his French toast.

Jesus Christ, I wanted to lick it off.

That would be inappropriate, though…wouldn't it?

"You have powdered sugar…" I gestured at my own face where it was on his, and he lifted his hand to swipe at his beard.

"I was saving it for later," he chuckled.

A grin stretched my mouth wide.

"That's acceptable, I guess," I said. "But I would hate for you to have pictures taken of you with food in your beard."

I gestured at the table behind us full of women who were talking about Hancock. They were whispering quietly, of course, but I'd heard them ask four or five times already if they thought it'd be okay to ask for a picture.

He glanced at the girls, then leaned over and tugged his wallet free from his pocket.

After fishing out two twenties, he tossed them on the table and held his hand out for me.

"Let's go," he ordered.

Instead of taking his hand, I hastily sucked down what was left of my coffee—*because hello! You don't waste coffee!* —and followed behind him as he rushed out the door.

He hadn't waited for me, so I had to rush to catch up, and I didn't miss the 'she's really fat for him' comment I heard as I passed by one table in particular.

And, apparently, Hancock hadn't missed it, either.

He stopped, turned, and headed back to the table that'd said the offending comment.

"What was that?" he asked the man who'd been unlucky enough to open his mouth.

I bit my lip, wondering if I should say it was okay or not.

But I chose to keep my mouth shut, because it sure as hell wasn't okay. Not even a little bit.

What if he'd said that to someone who wasn't like me? Who didn't let stupid comments like that go because they knew whomever had said it was just talking out of his ass?

Although I was confident in my body, I was also sensitive about it.

Had we been in a different situation and someone had said that about me, I'd have flipped out on their ass.

With Hancock here, though, I hadn't wanted to draw attention to the stupid man's comment.

Hancock, obviously, didn't have that same problem as me.

He lit into the guy with both barrels.

"I'm sorry," Hancock stopped at the table. "Did I mishear what you had to say?"

The man's mouth tightened.

"Because, if I'm not mistaken, I heard you call her a fat ass," he indicated me with a thumb. "I must've misheard, because surely you wouldn't call a woman as beautiful as she is fat."

My face heated.

"Fat is a relative term," the man said. "What's fat to me isn't going to be fat to you, obviously."

Hancock's brows rose.

"Is that right?" he asked. "And what makes you special? Why do you think it's okay to talk badly about women who you don't know?"

He was being incredibly calm about it, and I couldn't figure out why.

I could tell he was angry by the way he was holding his body. He was stiff and immobile. But if you were listening to his words and tone, you would think he was just having a conversation about everyday random things.

"I…" the man started, but Hancock held his hand up.

"All I want out of you is an apology, not an explanation," he grunted. "You may say it now."

The man glared but his eyes turned to me.

As insincerely as possible, he spat the words. "I'm sorry for calling you fat."

I nodded without saying thank you, because it was more than obvious that wasn't an apology.

Hancock realized that as well.

"This your daughter?" Hancock asked the man, indicating the little girl who was watching the discussion between the two men with avid, fascinated eyes.

"Niece," he murmured through pinched lips.

"And do you want someone saying that about your niece?" he challenged. "What would you do if some little boy came up to her and called *her* fat?"

"That's not very nice, Uncle Hammond," the little girl added her two cents.

Hancock's eyes filled with laughter as he looked at the little girl.

"No, Ma'am. It's not, is it?" he asked. "Have a good day, young lady. Stay out of trouble."

Those last two words I wasn't sure who they were focused on, but I assumed it was for the man and not the little girl.

Without another glance at the man, he turned on his heel and left the restaurant, leaving me once again to catch up.

"If you'd slow down, I wouldn't have to jog to keep up with you. Oh, and people wouldn't see things bouncing that shouldn't be bouncing!" I called to his back.

He slowed and turned, surveying my bouncing bits as he waited for me to catch up to him.

"Sorry," he muttered. "I hate taking photos."

"I noticed," I said. "You ready to go?"

He nodded.

"Yep," he sighed. "Have to be back for the game in an hour, and I need to drop you off and go back and get my stuff from my house."

"I'm not against riding with you if you want to run by there," I offered almost shyly.

He shot a small smile at me, and I had to take a deep breath as the full force of it hit me.

"It'll take half an hour to get there from here," he added as if he was making sure it was okay.

I nodded my head. "It's okay."

The second time I got into his big blue truck went better than it had the first time, on the way to breakfast.

He held the door for me while I placed one foot on the step. With one small jump, I heaved myself up into his truck, and wondered why on earth he had one so big.

He growled at one point, and I turned to survey him.

"Did you say something?" I questioned him.

His eyes went from where my ass had just been, to my face, and he shook his head.

"No," he said gruffly. "I didn't."

He slammed the door closed, and my brows furrowed as I watched him walk around the hood of the truck, and easily heft himself inside.

He didn't even need the handle like I did.

"I like your truck and all," I mused as he pulled into traffic and started heading in the opposite direction of town. "But it's impractical."

The corner of his mouth twitched as he chuckled softly.

"No," he smiled. "Not impractical. I'll show you why when we get to my place."

"Okay," I replied. "Why do you have to be at the stadium so early when the other players don't have to get there until one?"

He let his eyes flick to mine before returning them to the road.

"I don't, technically, have to be there until then, but I like to get there earlier," he hesitated. "It's a superstition."

"Mmmm," I murmured. "I know all about those *superstitions*."

"You do?" he asked in surprise.

"I do," I confirmed. "My brother is the king of superstitions. Although I don't see the point of them myself, I know what the thinking behind them is."

Hancock smiled as he pulled the wheel slightly to the left, taking the exit that would either lead to nothing, or Caddo Lake.

My guess was the lake, but he could surprise me and live in the middle of nowhere. Like a serial killer.

How much did I know about him?

Well, if I was being honest, I knew quite a bit. I knew his stats. His grade point average in high school. Oh, and I now knew he had a brother. But did that mean I knew him as a person? *No.*

I did trust him, though.

Even though he still made butterflies take flight in my belly every time he looked at me.

It was bad enough sitting in a confined space with him.

Adding in the fact that he smelled good had my hormones going haywire.

"What are some of your brother's superstitions?" he asked, startling me out of my reverie of his cologne.

"Uhhh," I cocked my head to the side and flicked up one finger. "He has to have on one specific pair of underwear, even if it's unwashed and stinky from the last game." I flicked up a second finger. "He has to drink a full bottle of red Gatorade, followed by only half a bottle of blue Gatorade."

He started to chuckle.

"He drinks the second half of the blue Gatorade only after he's won. If he didn't win, he throws the Gatorade away." I flicked up a third finger. "He shaves his head before each and every game."

"That's kind of the opposite of me," he fondled his beard. "After the first game, I don't shave anymore."

I noticed.

Everyone noticed.

By the end of the season, he was looking more like a homeless man than a baseball player.

He worked it, though.

"I think I noticed," I teased, turning in my seat to face him. "You won 'Baseball's Best Beard' last year on ESPN."

He rolled his eyes, his mouth quirking as he thought about what I'd just said.

"You've seen some of mine," he continued. "Have to sit in the same spot every game." He smiled but didn't look over at me. "I pull my pants up after my first at bat."

Yep, noticed that, too. Everyone did.

"You know that you have your own superstition Facebook page, don't you?" I inquired.

He chuckled as he made another turn, and my eyes went to the road we'd just taken.

"You live on the lake?" I asked.

"I do," he confirmed. "And Conner lives one house down from mine."

"Why do you live out here?" I asked.

"Because it's peaceful," he muttered. "And because I like to fish."

The loud sound of pipes had me looking at the road instead of him, and my eyes widened when I saw all the motorcycles parked outside one of the houses we were passing.

"What's going on there?" I whispered. "That doesn't seem very peaceful."

He grunted.

"It can get loud, but they're never rude about it. If it gets to be after nine in the evening during the season and I'm home, they'll walk their bikes in so they don't wake me," he winked. "I think they like me."

"Are they a club?" I probed, waving at the men.

Their eyes took me in, in the front seat of Hancock's truck, and all they did was nod.

Not one of them waved back.

Guess that wasn't a really biker thing to do.

"They're a club." He turned into his driveway, and my breath left me. "I'm not sure if they're good or bad, though. They like to have parties. I've gone to one or two since I've moved in, and nothing too illegal or too out of hand goes on at them."

"Hmm," I murmured. "Your house isn't on the lake…it's *on* the lake!"

He chuckled and opened his door, and I followed suit.

He rounded the truck just as I jumped down.

His hands on my hips startled me, and I looked up into his eyes with surprise.

"What…"

He slammed his mouth down onto mine, and I gasped, stealing his breath as I did.

His tongue took advantage of my opened mouth and plunged inside.

My hands went to his biceps, my tongue found his.

He growled as he pushed me back against the truck, and it took everything I had to stay upright as he took my mouth.

The moment he disengaged, I opened my stupid mouth.

"What was that?" I gasped.

He grinned.

"That…well, that's something I've been wanting to do for three freakin' days."

Hancock went on to have the best hitting game of his life…and guess what became his newest superstition?

CHAPTER 6

The only thing dirty about my beard is the mind that comes with it.
-Coffee Cup

Sway

"More ice?" I asked, taking glee out of the fact that each bucket of ice I added to Hancock's water made him shiver even more.

Today had been a practice day, and tomorrow would be a rest day, and the next day would be the actual game, and he'd practiced like shit today.

Though, I had a feeling that had a lot to do with the fact that he'd lost his catcher's mitt somewhere rather than him intentionally playing like shit.

"N-no," he said. "I think I'm getting sick."

My brows rose.

"You running a fever?" I asked.

Now that I was looking at him, he did look a little rougher than normal.

"T-think so." He nodded his head.

I reached down between his legs and started to pull the plug on the bath, but he stilled my arm.

"My thigh is fucking killing me from where I took that knee," he let my arm go. "I need the bath. *For now.* I'll get out in a few."

I watched as the color that was high on his cheeks that, earlier, I'd thought was due to the game, became more prominent.

Looking over at my assistant, Lacey, I beckoned her over with my hand. She was in the trainer program at a local college.

"Can you take a look at Gentry Green and make sure he's good to go?" I requested.

Lacey looked over at the bench that Gentry was sitting on, talking to another player, and then nodded. "I can do that."

She practically skipped as she rushed in his direction, and I had to hold my laugh in as she stopped directly in front of Gentry, completely blocking off the player he was talking to.

"She seems…excited," Hancock's rumble broke into my contemplation of how I was going to have to tell Lacey to take a chill pill.

"She's young and excited," I nodded my head. "I think she's going to turn into an awesome trainer…as long as we can get that starry-eyed look out of her eyes."

Hancock snorted, his eyes never opening.

"Where do you think you lost your glove?" I asked him, leaning against the tub as I stared down at him.

With his eyes closed, I admired his built chest and his tight, muscular thighs.

Most players wore their skivvies into the ice baths. Most.

Hancock usually didn't.

Today, though, he was still wearing his tight boxer briefs, not giving me the view of absolutely everything like he usually did.

However, it was enough.

Enough to heighten my breathing and make my face flush.

"Saw it in my locker before I went to eat after practice," he murmured. "And when I got back it was gone."

I pursed my lips.

"You think someone stole it?" I asked worriedly.

He cracked an eye open. "Yeah."

I frowned.

Stealing in professional baseball was nearly unheard of.

These guys had a lot of money and didn't *need* to steal.

If someone stole it, and he didn't just misplace it in a sickness-induced haze, then someone was about to get their ass kicked.

I had no doubt in my mind that Hancock would find his glove.

Hell, he'd hire a freakin' private detective and half the police force to find it if he had to.

Money, as I'd said, wasn't a problem for these boys.

Which made me wonder…why?

"Maybe you should start putting a lock on your locker," I suggested.

He grunted.

"I would…but numbers get fucked up in my head. I'm dyslexic," he muttered, sounding completely out of it. "Nine and six are a bitch for me to work with since they flop in my head."

He made a hand gesture to explain how they were switched around, and I felt a sweet sense of longing hit me.

"So, get one that doesn't have numbers, but a key," I suggested.

Hearing he was dyslexic tugged on my heartstrings.

He grunted. "I don't know what happened," he muttered. "But if it continues, then I'll get a lock."

"What if your batting gloves are taken next time…or your shoes?" I asked.

Lord knew his shoes were eight seasons old.

Well, likely they weren't eight seasons old. But it wouldn't surprise me if they were at least three.

He growled under his breath.

"I don't want to think about it," he muttered. "I'm trying not to die."

I covered a laugh by coughing into my hand, making him peak out between his eyelid again.

"Don't laugh at me," he ordered tiredly.

I patted his arm and walked around the tub.

"I'm getting a drink. Do you want anything?" I paused.

"Sprite."

I walked to the fridge I had in my office and removed my water. Then I grabbed a dollar from my wallet—which, might I add, was locked up in my freakin' desk—and got Hancock a Sprite from the drink machine before walking back to him.

He held his hand out before I was to him, and I had to wonder how he knew I was there.

"Will you open it for me?" he asked, turning the can's opening toward me.

I opened it without taking it from him, and wondered how, exactly, this kind of relationship between us had come to be.

Two weeks ago, when I'd started, if you'd asked me which player I would get closest to, I would *not* have said Hancock Peters.

I would've said none of them.

Why?

Because I was a social pariah.

I didn't talk to people easily. I didn't even talk to my own family easily.

Unless you asked me about a book, then I could talk to you like you were my best friend.

Which was how Ember had broken through my wall.

As for Hancock, I didn't know how he did it. Especially with how rude he'd been at the very beginning.

"Why don't you swing at the first pitch?" I asked him conversationally, taking a seat in the rolling chair and scooting closer to him.

I was worried if I didn't keep him awake, he could very well fall asleep in the ice bath, and then I'd be responsible for him drowning.

"Superstition," Hancock yawned, his mouth opening wide.

I resisted the urge to stick my finger inside his open mouth, and idly wondered if it'd piss him off if I did. By accident, of course.

I nodded my head as Gentry, Hancock's friend and tonight's starting pitcher, waved at me.

"You need a ride, big man?" he asked.

Hancock opened his eye slightly.

"No," he grumbled. "My truck should be back by now."

"It's not." He countered. "And seeing as it's after six, I doubt it's going to be back at all since the dealership closes at six."

Hancock cursed and pushed out of the water.

"Dammit," he growled.

My mouth went dry as I watched water sluice off his body in delicious waves.

Oh, my *tattoo*.

He had them everywhere.

I'd seen them, of course…*under the water.*

But since I was sitting directly next to him as he stood, I was close enough to actually feel the water dripping off his body.

And what a body it was.

So, *so* magnificent.

I lifted my hand and touched a tattoo on his hip of what looked to be a scratch mark of some kind. Then, where it looked like skin was ripped away, a grassy baseball diamond shown through.

"That's so cool," I mumbled, my eyes fascinated.

"I think she's actively trying to kill me," Hancock mumbled as he took the towel that Gentry offered him.

When he wrapped it around his waist, my hand got trapped in the material.

And, of course, that would be when my uncle came walking around the corner.

"Sway, do you think I could borrow you for a…" he stopped, and I yanked my hand away so fast it was more than obvious I'd been doing something inappropriate. "I thought I told you not to touch her, fool."

"Coach Siggy," Gentry was too busy laughing to try to conduct an understandable conversation.

I sighed.

"I wasn't doing anything," I promised.

"Uh-huh," Uncle Siggy murmured. "Sure looked like you were doing nothing instead of having your hand around his tattooed cock."

My mouth dropped open, and like always, my curiosity got the best of me.

"You have a tattooed weenie?" I exclaimed.

Hancock started to laugh, which died in his throat as coughing took over.

"What do you need, Uncle Siggy?" I asked, standing up and removing my hand from its confines.

Hancock walked out of the training room like he had lead weights tied around his ankles, and I couldn't help but watch as something foreign…almost like caring…filtered through my being.

"I need to borrow your phone." My uncle held out his hand while asking.

"What for?" I held onto my boob protectively.

It wasn't because Uncle Siggy had a code word for a boob named phone, but because that was where I held my phone while I was working.

It was stupid, I know. It was probably unsanitary, too, because of boob sweat, but that's where I kept it.

Not that anyone could notice.

My boobs were big enough to hide a fucking iPad, so concealing an iPhone was no problem.

He snapped his fingers. "Mine died. You know how Aunt Margaret gets when I don't call her on time."

"You mean when she starts accusing you of cheating on her?" I raised a brow at him as I offered him my boob-sweat covered phone.

He sneered slightly when I handed it off, but otherwise didn't comment about the fact that I'd had it stored in my bra.

"I'll be back," he muttered.

I rolled my eyes and started cleaning up, beginning first with the ice tub that Hancock had just exited.

Once the drain was pulled, I moved to the other tubs and wiped them down with disinfectant wipes before moving to the tables.

Once everything was clean and orderly, I snatched up my purse and keys, and headed to my uncle's office.

"No, I'm not with anyone else," Siggy mumbled under his breath. "Margaret. Jesus Christ. I'm at fuckin' work."

I rolled my eyes and walked up to Siggy, holding my hand out for the phone.

"Hold on," he mumbled, then handed it to me with a grateful look in his eyes.

"Aunt Marge," I interrupted the tirade I could hear coming through the phone without even having it up to my ear yet. "This is Sway. Uncle Siggy used my phone, but I have to go. I'll have to have him call you back later."

Without waiting for her negative response to my words, I hung up and dropped my phone into my purse.

"You really need to leave that woman, Siggy. That's not a healthy relationship," I admonished him.

"We have two kids together, a paid off house, and a grandkid on the way. Even if I did leave her, I'd still have to see her, so what's the fuckin' point of leaving her? At least, this way, I get regular sex," he explained.

I gagged.

"Gross," I grumbled. "Are you coming to dinner tomorrow?"

He gave me a look that clearly said he wasn't stupid.

"What?" I stifled a laugh.

"You damn well know I come to the dinners every Sunday night when I'm here," he grumbled. "Nobody can get out of it, not even me."

I agreed.

Every Sunday, Grams had a dinner that she expected every single one of her children and grandchildren to attend.

If they didn't, hell hath no fury and all that fun shit.

Grams was hell on wheels, and she would drive over to your house and yank your ass out of bed if that's what it took to get you there. On top of making everyone else wait.

I'd been on the receiving end of that quite a few times, and it'd gotten to the point where I knew better.

So did Siggy.

"Yeah," I sighed. "I'll see you tomorrow."

Exiting the office, I headed for the door that led to the employee parking lot, stopping the moment I made it out the door to find Hancock leaning heavily against my car. I continued to about midway into the lot before getting close enough to speak to him.

"What's going on?" I questioned him.

He looked up at me and studied me as I walked towards him.

"I want you to take care of me," he ordered once I was close enough to hear what he had to say. "I'm sick. Possibly dying."

I snorted.

"Why me?" I laughed.

"Because you'll actually take care of me," he smiled so pitifully that my lips twitched.

I rolled my eyes and walked to my car.

"Your house or mine?" I asked him.

I couldn't believe I was doing this.

I wasn't this type of forward girl, and I most definitely didn't bring men to my place very often…or at all.

In the end, the moment he got into my car, he passed out, and I chose to take him to my house.

Maybe he wouldn't notice that I was a crazy cat lady. Maybe he wouldn't care.

Maybe he found crazy cat ladies sexy.

CHAPTER 7

How do I stop eating chips and salsa? Do they run out or do I just die?

-Sway's secret thoughts

Hancock

"I'm dying," I muttered into the pillow, moving my face in between the beautiful pillows that felt like clouds.

The pillows that smelled like flowers and something else I couldn't quite identify.

Though that had a lot to do with the fact that my head felt like it was stuffed with cotton, and that I couldn't breathe through my nostrils.

"You're not dying," the angel of mercy whispered into my ear. "Are you going to play in your game today?"

I cracked my eyes open and stared at my angel.

"I like your eyes, Angel," I told her. "What are you doing in my bed?"

"You're in my bed," the angel corrected. "And you were in the other room up until about an hour ago. I'm not really sure why the hell you're in *my* room at this point."

She placed her hand in the middle of my chest and pushed.

Deciding to let her have her way, since she was an angel and all, I rolled over so I was no longer directly on top of her.

"I like your pillows," I muttered.

"Well, you gave my pillows beard burn," she grumbled. "Try not to put your beard on my breasts again, please. I think I'm allergic to your beard."

I grunted.

"Angels wouldn't complain about beards. You must be the devil," I moaned. "My head feels wonky."

"Your head is wonky," she shot back. "Otherwise you wouldn't think it's okay to sleep in my bed with your face between my breasts."

"Blasphemy."

When she laughed, I decided to show her what I meant and started to skim my hand up the angel's thigh.

"Stop." She slapped my hand away.

"If you were truly an angel, you'd give me the comfort that I want. Not turn me away," I grumbled, rolling until I was on my belly, my entire body curled up against the length of hers. "Keep me warm, Angel. I'm cold."

She said something under her breath that I couldn't hear, but I couldn't be bothered with such frivolities at this time. I was too tired.

My eyes closed, and I was dead to the world.

***

Sway

"Jesus," I yanked my arm out from under the big man. "You weigh a ton."

"Do not, Angel," he grumbled. "Your pillow's deflated."

I pulled until my arm was out from under his head, then rolled right on out of bed.

I couldn't handle his heat any more.

The man was fucking crazy active in bed, and I was literally exhausted from waking up not once, not twice. But over fifteen times since I'd gone to bed seven hours ago.

I'd woken up when he'd wormed his way into my queen-size bed and again when he'd rolled over on top of me and started using my breasts as pillows.

Then once more when he woke up shivering, and I'd stuffed Tylenol and ibuprofen down his throat.

Then he'd started sweating, drenching not just me but the bed, so I moved to the couch.

And he'd wound up on the couch, also.

It was like he was following me.

Using the time it took him to find me yet again, I quickly changed the sheets at four in the morning and got back into bed once more.

Now it was seven fifteen and he was, unsurprisingly, in bed with me.

Or was.

I'd had enough of being in bed with that man.

And sweet baby Jesus…the snoring!

I just hoped he didn't do that on a normal day when he wasn't sick.

The man sounded like a damn freight train.

If I hadn't been asleep before he'd gotten in bed with me, I would've found it really hard to even close my eyes with the sheer amount of noise he was making.

"Yo!" Someone pounded on my door. "Sway!"

I sighed and picked my pants up off the floor, thankful that Mr. McSnory Pants had been too under the weather to notice my state of undress.

Hopping on one foot, then the other, I worked my pants over my feet, then pulled them up before I got to the front door.

"Sway!" A man knocked hard again. "I know you're home! Open the goddamn door!"

Grimacing at the voice that was on the other side of the door, I contemplated whether or not to answer it or not.

There was a benefit to having my own home now.

I was an adult, and if I didn't want to answer the door, I didn't have to. Right?

But the more he pounded on my door, the more I realized he wasn't going to go away without talking to me.

Sighing in exasperation, I smoothed my hair back and reached for the knob.

"What do you want?" I asked the moment I got the door open.

My glare obviously didn't deter the man, because he pushed inside and tossed me a sneer as he did.

"I've been trying to call you," he said smoothly.

My brows rose.

"And?" I asked, crossing my arms over my chest.

His eyes went to my breasts, and he grinned.

I gritted my teeth and tried to force myself not to react to the stupid man's terror tactics.

Langston Spacey was my ex.

My ex-boyfriend. My ex supervisor. My ex-lover.

He was also my first.

He was also one of the worst mistakes I'd ever made in my life.

Things between Langston and I had started out awesome.

We'd met when I was trying to work myself through college.

He was the branch manager while I was only a lowly teller. We'd instantly hit it off, but I'd quickly found that Langston had two sides.

One side of his personality liked my curvaceous body. The other side despised it, especially when he had to take me out with his friends and introduce me as his girlfriend.

His mother also hated the fact that I couldn't find anything that didn't show off my 'ample attributes' or whatever the fuck that's supposed to be.

I could never tell if she was talking about the amount of breast I showed while dressed up, or the amount of rolls.

Either way I never received approval from his mom or him.

Two peas in a pod, those two were.

And I'd broken up with the certain 'pea' in front of me over a year and a half ago and had promptly moved out of the city.

This was my first time seeing him in all that time, and I didn't feel one single ounce of remorse.

None.

Not with Hancock currently in my bed only two rooms away.

"What do you want, Langston?" I asked carefully.

Langston narrowed his eyes at me.

"What's happened to you?" he asked, letting his eyes linger on my breasts once again.

I gained weight after we broke up, that's what happened.

Did I tell him that, though? Hell no. Then he'd just make a fat joke, and I'd heard enough of those to last me a lifetime.

"I wanted to ask you if you'd be interested in attending my work picnic." he cleared his throat.

My brows rose in surprise.

"I'm busy," I told him without hesitation.

"You don't even know what day it is," he countered.

I shrugged uncaringly. "It doesn't matter what day it is, I'm busy."

"I'd really like you to give us another chance." He took a step forward.

"Angel!" Hancock bellowed. "Where are you?"

"Who is that?" Langston stiffened, trying to walk past me toward my room like he'd done a million times, and I stepped in front of him.

"That is none of your business," I challenged. "Now please, I gave you my answer. You may leave."

He growled.

Langston was a big man.

He was perfectly coifed at all times, and today was no different.

I would shit my pants if the man ever let a whisker grow on his face.

He'd proven to me more than once that he was willing to shave twice a day so that he always looked clean-cut and presentable.

He also got his nails done once a month and made sure to always condition his hair for the recommended amount of time on the bottle.

I'd never seen him in anything that wasn't perfectly starched and pressed, and the one time I'd seen him get dirt on his shoes he had a freakin' conniption and demanded we go home immediately, even though we'd paid to go to the baseball game.

So yeah, all in all, Langston was a big ol' pansy.

"I'm not leaving until I know you're safe," he denied petulantly.

I nearly snorted my stray hair up my nose.

"You've got to be kidding me," I laughed.

"Kidding about what, exactly," he asked defensively.

My brows lowered.

"You really think you can protect me?" I snickered. "Langston, you'd have a cow if you ripped a shirt, let alone your skin. How do you think you'd defend me when you're too scared to get your hands dirty?"

Langston's eyes narrowed.

"Please, just go," I groaned. "This has been over for a very long time, and I don't want to deal with your shit right now. I'm starving and could really use a donut; not to mention I'm tired and irritable."

"You shouldn't eat donuts. They're not good for you. However, I'd be happy to take you to get a multi-grain bagel," he offered pleasantly.

I could do nothing but shake my head.

"It's like I'm talking to a brick wall sometimes," I muttered as I skirted around him, heading for the door. "Thanks for stopping by."

He didn't move from where he was standing in the middle of the room.

At least not until Hancock's angry, "She told you to leave," filled the room around us.

Langston's eyes widened at seeing the big man standing directly behind him.

Swear to God, the man moved like a cat! I hadn't even seen him arrive in the room, let alone creep up on Langston.

The differences between the two men were staggering. Even Hancock, who you could tell was sick as a dog, looked ten times better than Langston at his most pristine.

How had I ever found a baby face attractive? When it came to Hancock's beard, I was in love. The beard just made his already perfect self even more perfect.

Where Langston was soft, Hancock was rough.

Hancock had tattoos galore, where Langston wouldn't be caught dead looking like a 'hoodlum.' *His words, not mine.*

And from what I could remember, Langston had never looked like Hancock in his boxer briefs.

"Who are you?" Langston snapped, his chest bowing up in his perfectly pressed button-down dress shirt and purple striped tie that I'd bought him one year for his birthday.

Hancock's eyes narrowed.

"Why do you care?" he said pleasantly. "Angel, come back to bed."

A smile started to pull at the corner of my lips, and the words were out before I'd even meant them to come.

"You were moving like crazy and woke me up. I need donuts and coffee, stat," I shot back. "And, unfortunately, nobody's come up with a donut delivery, so I have to go get them if I want them."

He sighed. "I'll come with you. But after we're done, we're going back to bed with them."

I shook my head.

"Umm, hello," I snickered. "Glaze flakes in bed probably won't be very much fun to sleep on later."

"But imagine the possibilities when I lick them off your naked…"

"That is enough, Sir," Langston hissed, taking a step forward. "She is a lady, not a whore. Don't talk about her like that."

"I never said she wasn't a lady," Hancock shot back. "But a woman can be a lady in public and a whore in the bedroom if she damn well pleases. I'm up for anything Sway wants to give me."

By this point my jaw was likely down around my knees…or, at least, that was what it felt like.

To hear him talk about whoring and bedrooms was a sick sort of turn on, and I found myself wondering if being a whore in the bedroom was a good thing.

"Langston," I shook my head. "I think it's time for you to go now."

Langston turned his cold eyes on me.

"This isn't over," he assured me. "Not by a long shot."

"It'd be a long shot for you to ever get her back, so it's good you have the right mindset. You'll never win her back. Not with that attitude…and especially not since she now has me," Hancock grinned, making my heart flutter.

Langston headed for the door, but not before he stopped next to me and gave me his best glare.

"Your parents will be hearing about this…*caveman* in your house," he sneered. "And I'm sure your mother's going to love hearing about his filthy mouth." With that parting shot, he opened the door and left like his tail was on fire.

The grin that spread across my face was lighthearted.

"My mom has a thing about dirty mouths," I offered to Hancock who was looking at me to explain that last comment. "I'm sure you will hear about it very soon."

"How soon?" he countered.

I looked at my watch.

"Ohh," I pursed my lips. "I'll give it an hour."

I was wrong. It was forty-three minutes.

CHAPTER 8

No pants are the best pants.
-T-shirt

Hancock

My ass was dragging.

It literally hurt to stand, but upon hearing some other man's voice in the house I was sleeping in, I forced myself to get up.

Then I forced myself to walk into the unfamiliar living room and face off with a man who looked like a freakin' Sunday school teacher with his starched pants and button-down shirt.

Hell, even his tie was annoying with its stupid purple stripes.

I owned one suit and three shirts that could pass as dress up.

When I went out to formal events—which I tried really hard to get out of if it was at all possible—I got my personal assistant to find me something to wear.

This man, though? Yeah, he looked like he lived in formal clothes.

"Thank you," Sway smiled, interrupting my thoughts. "He's…difficult."

I snorted and moved to the couch, crumpling onto it the moment it was close enough for me to collapse on.

"Are you going to be able to play today?" she asked, looking at me warily.

I opened my eyes that I hadn't realized I'd closed and stared at her blankly.

"I don't have a game today," I said. "I have a game tomorrow."

"No," she shook her head. "You've been passed out for a day and a half. All day yesterday you did the whole fever, in and out of consciousness thing. Today is game day."

I groaned.

"I guess so," I muttered. "This should be fun."

"You know there's a backup catcher for a reason," she informed me.

I shrugged.

"Yeah," I said. "But even sick, I'm still better than him."

I snorted.

"Croft is good. In fact, given time, I think he could be excellent," she admitted. "You could be nice and show him the ropes. Teach him some stuff."

I gave her a look that clearly said what I thought about her opinion.

"And train him for my job?" I asked skeptically. "I think not."

She sighed and took a seat on the couch next to me.

"So I noticed your wall."

She promptly blushed profusely.

"I might or might not be your biggest fan."

I'd seen her Fathead of me on the way out the door to confront the douchebag.

It was a photo of me in my away colors, staring at the pitcher with a look of pure frustration and anger on my face. I remembered the game that it was taken at. I'd been hit twice each time I was at bat, and I was on ball three of four.

On ball four, I'd swung anyway. I'd connected with it, and had hit it straight out of the fucking park. The Fathead was of me, mid swing.

"It's okay," I said. "I just was surprised to see a life-sized sticker of myself on your wall, that's all."

And I was humbled.

That wasn't a new addition. Neither were the stats she had next to the sticker.

She liked me, and where it would've normally turned me off, it only turned me on more.

The proximity of her body to mine was amazing, and I wanted to reach out and run my hand along the exposed skin of her thigh.

She was wearing a pair of jeans, but those jeans had a hole in them from about an inch below her pocket all the way to the top of her knee. It was more than obvious that the distressed denim was meant to be that way, but my mind couldn't get over the fact that she had a hole in her jeans.

One very close to her crotch.

If I got overzealous, I could rip those fuckers from that hole all the way to her pretty pussy, follow suit with her panties, and bend her over before taking her from behind.

My cock started to stiffen, surprising me.

I was amazed that I could get it up with how truly shitty I felt.

None of my other body parts seemed to work, but, apparently, my cock functioned better than the rest of my body.

"You want anything for breakfast?" she asked when the silence continued.

"Donuts sounds good," I mumbled. "What time is it?"

"Ten."

My eyes snapped open.

"Mother fucker."

"What?" she asked in alarm.

"My dog. I need to go let her out." I started to get up.

She patted my hand.

"I called Gentry from your phone and asked him yesterday if he could take care of your dog," she soothed. "He took her home and brought you some clothes."

She looked pointedly at my boxer briefs, and her face started to flush pink.

The moment she touched my hand, I got harder. So, sue me.

What the hell did she expect? She was hot as fuck, and I wanted to fuck her. Tell my dick to behave around a combination like that.

"Donuts?" she squeaked.

I leaned forward, and then rocked twice before I found my way to my feet.

"Let me get dressed. Have I had any meds?" I asked on my way to her room.

"Your clothes are in the opposite room," she whispered. "And yes, you've had meds. But you're due for Tylenol and Ibuprofen in about forty minutes."

I looked at the other room she was indicating with her finger, and then smiled.

"Did I mention I sleep walk?" I asked, laughter filling my voice.

She rolled her eyes.

"No," she drawled. "I don't think you mentioned it." She smiled genuinely. "But I know...*now*. Turns out, I had to learn it the hard way."

***

Four hours later, I was warming up for the game.

I hadn't had the energy to practice beforehand, and my fucking glove was still missing.

Not to mention I still hadn't gotten a kiss from a certain someone.

"You look pretty puny today," Gentry observed as he walked up behind me.

Since Gentry had started last game, he couldn't start today. Meaning he wasn't dressed in his gear like everyone else.

Instead, he was in a blue warm-up slicker, his baseball pants, and tennis shoes.

"Thanks for bringing my shit and taking care of Ruby." I hopped up from my squatting position and rocketed the ball to second base.

My whole fucking body screamed as I did it, and I wondered idly if I'd be able to make it through the whole game.

When the coach went to toss me another ball, I waved him off.

"If I keep it up, I'll have nothing left for the game," I promised him. "I'm done."

The coach nodded, knowing not to bother arguing when I'd do what I wanted anyway.

"Maybe a donut will give you some energy?" Gentry offered his half-eaten donut.

I shook my head.

"I've already had two of Sway's donuts, which has definitely not been in my diet plan," I muttered. "Gonna be working that off for weeks."

Gentry snorted and turned to walk with me back to the locker rooms.

"Find your glove yet?" he queried.

I shook my head, anger flooding through me.

"No," I grumbled. "Coach is supposed to review the locker room feed, but since it was in the dressing area, it's not going to have it unless the fucker was stupid enough to walk out with it in his hands."

Gentry hummed.

"That is a pain in the ass," he said. "At least you have your backup glove."

At least.

Had I had to buy a brand new one, it would've been disastrous.

Breaking in a baseball glove took time. Time I didn't have when I was at the beginning of the season.

"I…"

"Hancock!" Sway called, interrupting what I had to say next. "I have a present for you!"

Sway's voice had a way of making me pay attention to her and only her. The moment I heard her call my name, every single cell in my body was quivering in anticipation.

"Yeah?" I asked.

She came to a stop in front of me, and then started digging through her bag.

"Couple of things, actually." She smiled at Gentry. "Hi, Gentry. I see you found the donuts."

Gentry hummed as he took another bite of said donut.

"Good, thanks. Shipley's makes my favorite kind." He shoved the rest into his mouth.

Sway smiled.

"Shipley's is everyone's favorite," I pointed out.

Gentry shrugged. "I'll talk to you in a minute. I want to talk to someone."

He left, and I watched as he walked to the reporter, Amity Lee, who was busy doing an interview with Furious George, our outfielder.

"Whatcha got for me?" I tried to peek into the bag.

She waved me into her office, and then closed the door.

The office was one of those with the glass doors, so although she'd closed it and nobody could hear us, they could most definitely see us, and not one of the players in the locker room made it a secret that they were watching us.

Furious George. Gentry. Rhys. Manny.

They were all watching, most of them chatting about what they thought was going on.

Turning my back to the door so I couldn't see them, and they could no longer see the desk since I was standing in front of it, I waited.

She didn't disappoint.

"I got you a few things to bring your energy levels up," she chirped. "You're not allergic to anything, are you?"

"Vicodin and Dilaudid," I answered. "And unless you have either of those things to give me, I think I'll be okay."

She grinned at me.

"That's definitely not one of my presents for you," she teased.

Then she held out a red Gatorade, a vitamin C supplement called Airborne, and a muffin.

"They're supposed to boost your Vitamin C and give you a little extra energy," she explained. "Kind of like having a Red Bull, but without the caffeine that'll make your heart race."

I nodded in understanding.

"How many of these do I take?" I asked, holding up the vitamin C supplements.

"The bottle says you can take up to four," she explained. "But I usually take three, and I feel a difference. You're not much bigger than me…"

I gave her a look that clearly said to shut up, and she snapped her mouth closed.

"Four," she reiterated.

I grinned and opened the bottle, popping four of the most disgusting pills that I'd ever tasted.

"Gross," I gagged as I washed them down with the Gatorade. "Thank you."

She waved away my thanks.

"The muffin is good, but it might take some time to eat it all. It's really rich." She gestured to the last thing in my hand.

I peeled the wrapper off it and took a large bite.

The flavor burst in my mouth, and I contemplated moaning as the most delicious thing I'd ever tasted made its way down my throat.

"This is good," I told her. "Did you make this?"

She shook her head. "No. My mom did."

I moaned and took another bite, my eyes popping open wide as I stared at the little crack-filled muffin.

"This is probably going straight to my ass," I mumbled just before taking another bite. "It tastes like chocolate cake."

"It's more like a brownie cake, icing drizzled all over type of thing. Although there is some protein powder in there," she added.

I smiled. She started to giggle at what I was sure were my teeth. I couldn't find it in me to care at that point, though.

"She should go into business making these," I muttered. "I'd buy one a day if she did."

Sway laughed and tapped the paper that the muffin had come in.

"She does." She pointed at a sticker that was wadded up. "She owns *It'll Do Bakery and Treats* on Tyler Street."

"That place is new, isn't it?" I asked.

The reason I knew anything about it at all was I'd seen an ad next to an article I'd been reading in the sport's section in the newspaper. What had held my attention, though, was that she specialized in products directed more towards athletes.

Sway nodded. "She opened up a couple of months ago, but already she's done better than anyone expected her to. Though that might have a lot to do with the fact that my brother is a major league baseball player, and in the paper, they may have mentioned that fact."

I shrugged. "Whatever works, I say."

She grinned.

"Your head feeling any better?" she questioned.

I shook my head, and now that she'd drawn attention to the fact, I could say that I didn't feel any better at all.

"Not even a little bit," I admitted. "Fucking headache from hell. Who the hell gets colds like this during the summer?"

Her lip quirked up.

"Obviously, you do," she pointed out.

"Yo, Sway!"

I turned to find Ronnie Hamels, one of the relief pitchers, come up to Sway with a look of adoration on his face.

It took everything in me not to snarl at him in annoyance.

"Yes, Hamels?" she smiled sweetly.

"I need you to wrap my wrists, please." He showed me his hand. "Is that okay?"

He looked back and forth between Sway and I, and I had to sigh in understanding.

"We're not busy," I informed him. "Thank you, Sway. The muffin's good. And the Gatorade, as well."

She smiled happily.

"I'm glad. Don't forget to take your meds, okay?" she pushed. "And you can have that every six hours." She pointed at the meds. "Promise. They may taste like crap, but they're worth it."

With that last parting comment, she patted Hamel's shoulder and started walking into the training room, leaving me staring after her as the two of them spoke more easily than Sway and I ever had.

What I didn't see, though, was sexual attraction.

At least I had that going for me.

Maybe I was closer than I thought I was.

***

An hour and a half later, I was suited up and ready to go on the field. The only thing missing was my glove and my kiss…both of which I wanted more than my next breath.

The glove because I just plain wanted my glove back. It was mine and somebody took it from me. They violated my privacy, stole my property and nearly ruined my hitting streak.

My kiss was important because the game that I'd first kissed Sway had been the first game in a long time when I got on base every single at bat.

And since only two things had changed, and only one of those things had been a good thing, I knew exactly what I needed to do.

Which was why I was winding through the halls of the complex looking for a slippery brunette with curves that set my blood on fire.

"Excuse me," I stopped a janitor. "Have you seen the athletic trainer? Medium height," I gestured with my hand to my shoulder. "Curvy. Big…"

"If you say tits, I will kill you," Sway said with amusement from in front of me.

I snorted and turned, totally dismissing the janitor as I took in Sway from in front of me.

Today, she was in khaki pants that fit her like a second skin, showing off all of her generous curves so perfectly that I had half a mind to take a picture so I could use it as my wallpaper.

That might be a little too much for her at this point, though, so I reigned myself in and took in the rest of her attire.

Her top half was covered up by a green and white polo—the

Lumberjacks' colors—that was so tight that her breasts strained the material and made the buttons struggle to hold her shirt closed.

Then there was the hat, hiding the upper half of a complicated French braid that looked like it'd take a million years to do.

It was one of those hairdos like one would see on a bride at her wedding. Not the normal kind of French braid that I'd always seen.

"I like your hair," I blurted.

Her face flushed.

"What can I help you with?" She started to walk past me.

I moved so that I was in step next to her, keeping the same pace she was as we started to wind our way back to the top of the complex.

"I wasn't gonna say your tits were big," I informed her, rubbing my beard.

"Then what were you going to say?" She waited.

I smiled and let her think it was something bad, but in all reality, it wasn't. Not even a little bit.

When she made an impatient sound, I decided to put her out of her misery.

"Your eyes," I said with a chuckle.

She rolled those big blue eyes toward me with calculation in their depths, and I stared right back, letting her see the sincerity in mine.

"You're bad," she sighed. "But really. What was it you needed from me?"

We'd just topped the last set of stairs, and I stopped her with a hand on her arm before she could open the stairwell door that would lead to the training room as well as the locker room.

Her eyes widened when I crowded her body close.

"What are you doing?" she asked worriedly, frantically trying to push me away from her.

"I'm doing what I've got to do," I told her.

"And what, exactly, is it that you 'got to do'?" she asked warily.

"I've got to win," I pointed out. "And to win, I have to collect on my kiss."

She licked her lips nervously. "That's probably not why you won last game."

I looked at her.

"Someone stole my glove," I told her.

She nodded.

"Yeah, so?" she shivered when I moved my hand up to cup her elbow.

My hand traveled up her arm, disappearing underneath the sleeve of her polo shirt as I explained.

"My glove was stolen. I was sick. And I had a high potential of having a really shitty game," I pointed out.

"Uh-huh." Her eyes were heavy lidded as I let my fingers trail along the strap of her bra.

My hard body pushed into her soft, pliable flesh from breasts to knees, and she started to breathe heavier. Her breasts rising and falling with each inhale and exhale.

"What I'm trying to say," I murmured. "Is that it could have been very bad. But it wasn't…because of one single thing."

Her eyes found mine and I started to lower my head.

"And what was that?" she whispered.

I smelled the cinnamon before I tasted it on her lips, and the moment our flesh met, I knew that things would never be the same.

I'd kick ass at this game, and any other game, if she was there to do this one single thing for me each and every time I played.

Knew it with as much surety as I was sure I'd draw my next breath.

Her hands found my shoulders, and then went even further to wrap around my neck as she leaned into the kiss.

But before it could get too out of hand, the door beside us slammed open, and would've hit us had I not caught it before it could.

Luckily, the door hid us from view, because as I moved my face away from hers, licking my lips as I went, I knew it would've been more than obvious what we were doing.

Her face was red from my beard. Her lips swollen.

Her eyes were glazed, and her breathing was still heavy.

She was the epitome of aroused.

She didn't hide her feelings at all.

"Gotta go, Half-Pint," I touched her nose. "See you in the dugout."

With those last words, I let the door go, moved around it, and then jogged down the long hallway that led to the locker room.

And the entire freakin' way I had to force myself not to turn back.

She was addicting indeed.

CHAPTER 9

I've decided I'm an ass girl. Horses are majestic as shit, but they don't have the redeeming qualities that a donkey has.
-Sway's twisted thoughts

Sway

I couldn't stop thinking about that kiss.

Every single time I would let my mind wander, it inevitably went back to it.

Now, the problem was knowing what was under that hard body I'd been running my hands all over during that kiss.

A kiss that was three hours, one minute and thirty seconds ago.

A kiss that rocked my world.

A kiss that I wanted to repeat…over and over and over again.

"Hancock 'Parts' Peters, number 49, has been on fire tonight. I heard from another player that he was under the weather, but you wouldn't be able to tell from this performance," the announcer for Fox Sports, repeated for the fifth time. "He is on fire! Rose, replay the play from earlier."

They replayed the play, again, and I watched, again, as Rhys caught the shallow pop fly to left field. The runner on third took off once the ball was caught and went for home. Rhys threw the ball home and, the runner realizing his mistake once he saw Hancock catch the ball, lowered his shoulder and ran into Hancock like a battering ram.

Both Hancock and the player went down in a tangle of limbs.

Poor Hancock was slow to get up, but get up he did…with the ball securely in his glove despite the pained grimace on his face.

Everyone but Hancock celebrated—including me.

"Yo," Coach Siggy called. "You're up!"

I turned to survey the sweaty man beside me, and barely managed to look down at my hands in time to avoid making eye contact with him.

I knew if I made eye contact with him, my entire face would flame. Which wouldn't be good seeing as everyone—the press, the cameras, the fans, his teammates—had been watching every single move Hancock made for the last six innings.

"Let's get a couple of runs," Siggy called out.

I bit my lip and lifted my head to watch him as he made his way out to the field, his wooden bat in his hand, resting against one shoulder.

"What do you think he's going to get this time?" Gentry asked from the seat beside me.

I knew he was talking to me.

He'd been doing it the entire game just to piss Hancock off.

Each time he'd say something, he'd turn to Hancock to gauge his reaction, and I was beginning to wonder if I should be answering his questions if it was pissing Hancock off each time I answered.

Eventually, I'd gotten up and moved to the end of the dugout.

Which had pissed Hancock off even more.

With one pointed glare in my direction and a gesture for me to retake my seat, I sighed and moved back.

Superstitions! What the everloving fuck was wrong with these men?

"I'm going to guess a home run."

I was a glass half full kind of gal. If I could have it any way, I was going to go all in.

If I had to bet, I'd bet every single cent I had on me.

Most of the time that resulted in me losing my money in the first forty seconds, but that was the way I was.

All or nothing.

Which happened to be why I was letting Hancock do what he wanted to, and damned the consequences.

That'd always been my downfall.

I…

"Holy shit," Gentry swore.

My head whipped around to the plate to see Hancock peeling himself off the ground, a glare on his face aimed at the pitcher.

"What happened?" I asked worriedly.

"Pitcher was going to walk him, so he was throwing the ball outside," Gentry explained. "When Hancock crowded the plate to get access to the balls, the pitcher threw one down the middle and nearly took out his knees."

My brow lifted.

The pitcher must be stupid, I surmised.

Otherwise, he would've never tried to hit Hancock.

Hancock was known as a hothead.

It didn't take much to get him going.

Sure, he'd mellowed with his age, but most pitchers knew better than to taunt him. If you kept the beast soothed, then it was likely he wouldn't go all crazy on your ass.

This kid, though…well, he was *new*.

That was my only hope for why he did what he did next.

"Crowding the plate again," Gentry murmured. "Shit, did you see the look he just gave that pitcher? How is he not shitting his pants right now?"

"Maybe he did. I would have," Rhys, the third baseman, pointed out.

Chuckles filled the air, and then all breath left every single man's body in the dugout…hell, in the entire freakin' stadium.

The ball left the pitcher's grip, and I knew it was going to hit him. I was so certain that I was already up and moving out of the dugout before Hancock had even finished falling to the ground.

Taking a pitch to the throat was going to hurt on the best of days. Taking a ninety-eight mile an hour fastball to the throat was a completely different story.

I hit my knees beside Hancock's gasping form and carefully rolled him over to his back.

His hands were on his throat as he struggled to breathe, and I latched onto his face with one hand as I tugged my bag closer with the other.

I yanked out my portable oxygen tank, and immediately strapped it onto his face as I looked into Hancock's tear-filled eyes.

The big man was looking at me with so much fear that it was hard to keep calm and not whisper that it would be okay.

A paramedic dropped down next to me.

"He was struck in the neck with the ball," I told him.

I wasn't a medic.

Hell, I wasn't the type of medical professional that Hancock needed at this point, but I couldn't force myself away.

Even if I could have, I wouldn't have been able to leave. Hancock's grip on my thigh was to the point of pain he was holding on so tightly.

"He needs to go to the hospital," the medic murmured. "Where's the... ahh, there it is."

I turned to see the gurney on the way toward us, and I turned back to Hancock whose eyes hadn't left mine.

"They're going to take you to the hospital," I told him. "You need to go with them and not give them any lip."

I started to back away to give the other medics room, but he snatched my hand in a move of desperation that pleaded with me to stay.

"His breathing's better, but his O2 sats are still low," the medic murmured.

"He's sick," I informed them. "He had a fever and started coughing about thirty-six hours ago."

The medic nodded.

"Let's hope that's the reason for the low sats then," he murmured. "You going with us?"

I stood up as the gurney slid into the space beside Hancock.

His breathing was still rough and choppy, and I knew it pained him to breathe.

The ball had glanced off the front of his throat, luckily only grazing off of him when he lifted his shoulder at the last moment.

But the hit was enough to make his throat begin to swell.

Hits to the neck are always serious injuries and can even be fatal sometimes. If there was damage to his airway—like we suspected there may be—or the injury was to the back of the neck, affecting the brain stem, then it could be really dangerous.

"I'm going," I nodded.

Turning I found my assistant standing behind me.

"Can you take over here?" I asked her.

She nodded quickly. "I have the others, too."

She gestured to the other trainers who'd stayed away to let the medics do their job.

"Good," I nodded. "Call me if you need me."

She nodded quickly again, and I turned to start walking with the medics.

Which turned into a run when Hancock's O2 sats fell even lower.

His eyes, though, before he passed out…*they would haunt me for the rest of my life.*

***

I crossed my arms as I waited in the ER waiting room.

We'd been separated for over an hour, and I was getting antsy.

The waiting room had filled so full that I was actually now in the hallway leading into it.

There were people crowding the halls who were fans, and there were even more fans outside!

Seriously…it would've never occurred to me to come to see a man—

baseball player or not—if I didn't know him personally.

"Any news?" Uncle Siggy asked as he walked up to me, looking so tired he could barely stand.

I shook my head. "Nothing."

"You think he's going to be okay?" He took up position against the wall next to me to wait.

"Yes." I knew he'd be 'okay.' Whether 'okay' meant he could play baseball again was another thing. "He turned blue in the ambulance, and they almost had to trach him."

Siggy's mouth went tight.

"They gave him some kind of anti-inflammatory med and were able to obtain a clear airway about thirty seconds after that," I continued. "I'm not sure what that means for now, though."

"Sway Cooper?" a nurse called.

My body jolted, and I immediately started walking over to the woman.

"I'm Sway," I told her eagerly. "Is he okay?"

The nurse smiled. Well, I was sure she'd intended it as a smile, but it came out more like a grimace.

"He's asking for you." She smiled at my uncle, who I could feel at my back, then returned her eyes back to me. "If you'll follow me."

I waved at my uncle and he nodded his head. "Call me when you find anything out."

I nodded my head back at him and hurried after the woman.

She was a long-legged blonde with curly hair and a nice, perky ass.

"His room is right there," she pointed.

"Thank you," I dismissed her without a second thought.

The moment I breached the door, Hancock's eyes turned to me, and then he breathed an audible sigh of relief.

The first thing I noticed was that he wasn't on a ventilator, and he didn't have any new holes in his neck.

The second thing I noticed was that he was naked from the chest up with blankets covering his lower half.

I momentarily lost my way and stared at his defined chest, before a rough, deep chuckle had me snapping back to attention.

"Hancock!" I cried. "You scared the fucking hell out of me!"

He held his hand out for me to take, and I latched onto that strong, masculine hand like it was my lifeline.

"They tried to cut my beard," he muttered.

I didn't point out that they *did* cut his beard.

Instead, I studied his throat, and the purple and blue bruising under his skin.

"So, what's going on?" I asked. "Are you okay?"

"He's doing great," a doctor came in behind me. "He's responding well to the anti-inflammatory meds we put him on. We're just waiting for the results of the MRI and CT scan. As long as they come back clear, then he'll be free to leave in another couple of hours."

I turned my gaze away from the doctor to stare at Hancock.

"We're worried, though, that he might have strep. However, we're treating that with some antibiotics," the doctor continued.

"If you gave me strep, I'm going to throw up all over your carpet," I warned him.

Hancock's mouth tipped up at the corner.

"Why be so specific?" he asked.

"Strep makes me puke...every single time," I informed him. "And you'll have to take care of me because I turn into an invalid," I grinned. "Kind of like you did yesterday."

His eyes shone with amusement.

"I'm actually surprised he was able to make it through the entire game without collapsing in exhaustion," the doctor observed. "I was watching the game. He was amazing right up until that kid hit him."

Hancock's mouth tightened.

"Kid's going to get his ass kicked the next time I see him," he muttered. "Am I free to play at the game two days from now?"

Did he sound hopeful?

"Honestly," the doctor hesitated. "I would give it a game. But if you can find a neck guard to play with for the next couple of games, and you're feeling up to it, then I would say I think it'll be alright...as long as your tests come back all clear."

I grinned.

"Thank fuck," Hancock smiled. "That's the best news I've had in the last hour."

The doctor left after giving his instructions while we were waiting on results, and I sat on the corner of Hancock's bed.

"Can you turn that on?" He pointed to the TV.

I nodded, knowing he was looking for a recap of the game.

Not needing to be asked, I found the remote, turned the TV on, and found Sports Center without a word.

And, of course, the game's highlights were on while a couple of analysts discussed the game.

"There have been other men hit in the neck before," one of them said. "It's a very dangerous area to be taking a hit."

"Thank you, Captain Obvious," Hancock muttered. "Show the replay."

"It is, Pat," the other man said. "From what I could tell, as they took him off the field, he was breathing, which was one of the main concerns."

I rolled my eyes and continued to watch, standing next to Hancock's bed.

"Here it is," I turned it up.

We watched the confrontation before the hit, and then the hit itself, in silence.

Only after it was done did Hancock find his voice.

"Was there a fight?" he asked.

I turned to look at him.

He was staring at the TV with a whimsical look on his face.

"I don't know." I admitted. "I was with you. Though, from what I heard from the assistant trainers and the state of some of the players' faces and knuckles, it seems that there was."

Hancock grinned.

"Can you give me a drink of that?" He pointed to the small cup with a white bendy straw in it.

I immediately got it for him and brought the cup to him.

Instead of taking it, though, he leaned forward and drank it directly from my hand.

His throat worked, and his eyes closed as the cool water soothed his throat, and I realized two things.

One, the man was sexy, even bruised up and hurt.

Two, I was falling in love with him.

Out of all the people he could've called back for, he'd asked for me.

That was saying something.

Maybe he wasn't just playing around.

Maybe—just maybe—he really was serious about me. Maybe he really did want me.

The real question was if I could let my walls down long enough to let him in.

And looking at his face, the gratitude in his eyes, I realized that I could.

I could do anything for him.

CHAPTER 10

The problem with reaching for the stars is that it leaves your balls unprotected and vulnerable. Trust me, I know. FYI – my brothers are douches.
-Hancock's secret thoughts

Hancock

I was sitting comfortably in my La-Z-Boy recliner, my eyes closed, and Sway humming along in my kitchen when I heard it.

It was a distinct sound.

Really distinct.

The sound of keys in my door.

My eyes snapped open and I glared at the doorknob, hoping beyond hope it wasn't who I thought it was.

But, like always, I wasn't given the reprieve I needed.

My brothers, three out of the four of them, walked in the next moment, followed shortly by my parents.

"Oh, baby," my momma cried as she rushed to me. "Your throat looks horrible!"

I barely resisted the urge to sigh.

She would catch it, and then she would get all hurt that I wasn't letting her mother me like I 'should' be letting her. It was her God-given right, after all.

Something she told me all the time when I refused her attentions.

"I have strep throat," I told my brothers. "I hope you all get it."

Harrison, Holden and Hunter all stared at me.

"Where do you think you got it from, dumbass?" Harrison asked.

I gritted my teeth.

"Y'all know damn well y'all are supposed to stay the fuck away from me when you're sick," I growled. "This could've been detrimental."

"You look like you're running a fever right now," my mom, Sally, frowned. "I'm going to go make you some chicken noodle soup."

She froze when I said what I said next.

"My woman's in there making me soup."

She turned only her head and stared at me with frightening eyes.

"Woman?" she asked carefully.

I nodded my head, wincing when the movement caused my head to hurt even more than it was already hurting.

"When did you get a woman?" Holden asked skeptically.

"Oh," Sway gasped in surprise. "Hello!"

I turned to find her standing in the doorway to the kitchen, her eyes taking in my brothers and my parents in one long sweep.

Then without pausing, she walked into the room and over to me, setting a steaming bowl of French onion soup—her specialty, she'd assured me—

on the coffee table in front of me.

"My name's Sway," she held her hand out to the closest brother, which happened to be Hunter.

My mom had five boys, Harrison, Holden, Hunter, Hannibal and then me. She had us all one right after the other, starting with Harrison and ending with Hannibal and I, who were identical twins.

Hannibal and I were the only ones left who weren't married with kids. I was the only one who hadn't experienced psycho mom when it came to my serious girlfriends because I never had serious girlfriends before.

Never wanted them.

Until Sway.

Now I wanted a lot of things, most of those things being Sway in my bed, naked underneath me.

Forever, if possible.

But I hadn't told her that yet. I wouldn't be. Not until she was well and truly trapped.

If it wasn't immoral and a tad bit archaic, I'd just get her pregnant and play on her conscience to stay with me for the rest of her life.

I knew I could make her happy.

Hell, I knew she made *me* happy.

"Well, hello!" Hunter drawled, taking her hand in his and caressing the outside of it while he stared into her eyes. "Aren't you pretty?"

She blushed and pulled on her hand, and my brother had no other option but to let it go or look like a creepy motherfucker.

So, he chose to let it go.

That didn't stop him from moving closer to her.

"Hunter," I growled. "I'll tell Stella that you couldn't keep your hands to yourself," I warned when Sway moved to my father.

Hunter shot me a grin, but he backed up until he hit my chair, and then slammed his hip into it.

I grunted as pain burst through my body.

"Fucker," I grumbled, my hand going to my neck in reaction.

My mother's eyes were glaring daggers at Sway as she moved from person to person, introducing herself.

"Isn't it kind of rude that you're not introducing us?" Harrison drawled from where he was standing next to my mom.

I sighed, long and loud, and turned to Sway.

"That's my mom, Sally. My brothers, Harrison, Holden, and Hunter. And that man you're standing next to is my pop, Drake."

Sway's smile was brilliant.

"It's nice to finally meet you," she said genuinely. Then ruined it with a lie. "Hancock's told me so much about you."

I barely contained the urge to snort.

Instead, I busied myself with leaning forward and eating the soup she'd made.

My diet was shot to hell this week, and I promised myself that I'd try to do better.

"Darling, do you need some bread with that?" my mom asked.

I had just opened my mouth to reply to that when Sway jumped.

"Oh!" she clapped. "My mom brought some of hers over earlier. Let me go get you some."

My mother glared at her back the entire way into the kitchen.

Once she was completely in the kitchen, the questions started.

"When did you meet her?" Hunter asked.

"Where did you meet?" Holden questioned.

"She's cute," my father grinned.

"Isn't she the athletic trainer I saw helping you when you got hit in the throat at the game?" Harrison asked.

"What is she wearing?"

That was my mother.

I turned to survey my mom.

"She's wearing jeans and a t-shirt. What does it look like she's wearing?" I snapped at her.

My mother sniffed.

"I can see too much cleavage," she hissed.

I rolled my eyes, which only seemed to infuriate her more.

"Don't roll your eyes at me, boy." She pointed her finger at me. "I'll have you know that I brought you into this world, and I sure can take you out of it."

Holden laughed, as did my dad.

"Take a chill pill, Sally," my father said as he took a seat on the couch and lifted his feet to the coffee table I was eating on.

"Dad, you have cow shit on your boots," I told him. "Please remove them from my face."

Dad didn't remove his boots.

He never did.

Everyone, even me, was used to cow shit.

When you owned a ranch, shit was normally part of the equation.

It just wasn't in my fucking house, which was why I picked my soup up and walked to the bar that separated the kitchen from the living area.

Each step I took jarred my head.

My throat felt like fire, and my eyes were getting heavy.

I would eat, though, because I knew if I didn't, I'd likely wake up in the middle of the night starving.

The moment I sat down I could see into the kitchen, and my head tilted as I watched Sway stare blankly out the window. Her eyes watched the river flow, and I wondered if she liked my sanctuary as much as I did.

Then a rough cough tore from between my lips.

"Oh," Sway jumped, startled when she turned around. "I was just about to bring this out to you."

She held up a couple of slices of bread.

"Just one, please." I held out my hand for it. "I'm not sure I can swallow it."

She smiled and came unstuck from where I'd caught her contemplating the lake.

"What's wrong?" I asked once she was close enough.

She shook her head, and before she could retreat from handing me my bread, I grabbed her hand and pulled her to me.

She couldn't get very close, but it was close enough that I didn't worry that my family would overhear what I had to say next.

"Tell me what's wrong," I demanded gruffly.

She pursed her lips.

"I just think it's time for me to leave," she admitted. "Now that your mom is here, I don't think you need me anymore."

"Do you need to leave?" I tilted my head.

She shook her head. "No."

"Do you want to leave?" I continued.

She shook her head, not replying this time.

"Then stay."

"But your mom," she whispered, looking over my shoulder. "She doesn't look like she wants me here."

"My mom's like this with all the new women that enter her boys' lives," I told her bluntly. "It's like she wants to test their will or something. See if they have any gumption."

I had no doubt that, by the end of the night, Sway would have my mother wrapped around her finger.

Sway was easily the funniest and sweetest woman I knew.

Not to mention she wasn't a gold digger like the rest of the ladies I met nowadays.

I'd never met someone that I wanted to spend more time with…not until Sway.

When I woke up in the hospital and saw that she was no longer with me, I demanded for her to be brought back to me for over thirty minutes.

The only reason she had been brought back to me was after the doctor overheard. Then he'd intervened on my behalf and demanded the nurse go and get 'my fiancée.'

Not that Sway had heard that little tidbit.

"Hey," Holden called as he marched up to my side. "Do you have any extra of that?"

He pointed to my soup, and she nodded.

"I do. Do you want some?" she asked.

"Yep." He sat down. "Order up."

I elbowed Holden in the ribs and gave Sway an apologetic look.

"My brothers are heathens," I told her. "Ignore them if you need to."

She grinned, but got my brother some soup, and then sliced him off his own slice of bread before placing both in front of him.

I took a sip of my own soup as I tried hard to swallow it.

It wasn't that it was bad. It was that my throat hurt like a motherfucker.

Even water was a killer to swallow.

"Do I have any ice cream in that freezer?" I asked Sway.

She shrugged and turned, presenting me with her lush ass as she bent over and looked into the pullout freezer.

Never before had I wanted to give an appliance a hug, but there was certainly a first time for everything.

She nodded and unearthed a carton of Blue Bell Great Divide, which was a Texan's term for chocolate and vanilla, and set it on the counter.

"Which kind do you want?" she asked me, raising her eyebrows in question.

"Both," I said. "Otherwise they'll be uneven, and I'll have to buy a new carton."

She looked at me strangely, and I crossed my arms as I waited for what I knew was coming.

"That's the oddest thing I've ever heard," she finally said. "But it's not unusual. My brother does the same thing. We call him the Divide King."

I snorted and watched as she struggled to spoon the ice cream out.

"Can you help her, dillweed?" I nudged my brother.

Holden sighed long and loud, but got up and easily scooped the ice cream out.

"Can I have some, too?" Sway's eyes were pleading.

Holden nodded and started scooping again.

After two scoops, one from each side, she held her hand up.

"That's enough," she ordered. "If I have more than that, it'll go straight to my hips."

My eyes went down to the hips in question and I barely contained the urge to moan.

Even sick as a dog, she had a way to make my dick hard.

"Well, if Holden's passing out ice cream, I want some!" Harrison yelled loudly as he walked around the counter into the kitchen.

He walked straight to the cabinet with the bowls, lifted another out, and then held it out to Holden.

Holden ignored him as he left the spoon where it was and went to the sink to wash his hands.

"Asshole," Harrison growled.

"I don't know how your mother does it," Sway interrupted Harrison's fit. "Y'all all look so much alike. I'm already lost on who's who."

"I do it because I know my kids," my mother sniffed, placing her hand on my back. "And I've got about thirty years of experience on you."

I was glad to see that my mother was at least addressing Sway now, but that might have a lot to do with the talk I could hear my father having with her while I was trying to choke down the soup.

"You don't like your soup?" my mom asked hopefully.

I nodded my head.

"I like it," I told her. "But it hurts to swallow it. I'm going to try ice cream."

She patted my back like I'd done the right thing. I was sure it was more because she was happy I wasn't enjoying the soup that Sway had made especially for me.

"Oh, my God," Holden moaned. "This soup is the bomb!"

My mother's hand stopped patting my back, and I could see out of the corner of my eye that she was now glaring at Holden.

"You should try this, y'all," Holden urged. "I've never tasted anything so good in my life. And this bread is to die for."

"You sound like you're having an orgasm," Harrison muttered. *"Oh, God. It's so good! Harder, Sway!"*

I stopped with my spoon halfway to my mouth, dumped the ice cream back into the bowl, and launched the spoon at my brother's head.

It hit him in the forehead, causing him to cry out, but continue to laugh.

"Oww!" he yelled between bellows of laughter. "You asshole! I was only teasing!"

I rolled my eyes and took the spoon that Sway handed me.

"To be honest," Sway surmised as she looked at the welt rising up on my brother's head. "I would've left the ice cream on it when I threw it. At least he did you that favor."

I winked at Sway, then returned to licking my ice cream.

"Well…" my dad said. "I have to take a shit, so I'll let y'all deal with this while I commune with the gods."

I closed my eyes as a laugh built in my throat.

When I opened my eyes again, it was to find Sway's smiling eyes on me.

"If you think this is bad…" she grinned. "I can't wait for you to meet *my* family."

CHAPTER 11

It's only an extra bottle of beer if you don't drink it.
-Hancock's words of wisdom

Hancock

"Your brother's name is 'Holden Peters.'" She stared at me, her face cracking into a grin.

I snorted.

"Yeah, my parents weren't really thinking that through at the time, were they?" I asked as I sat down onto the bed.

"You need any help?" she bit her lip.

I shook my head.

"No," I leaned back slowly until my head hit the pillow, my whole body protesting the movement.

"Alright," she said as she came to my side of the bed and stood over me. "Gentry texted you to say he'd bring your dog home in the morning."

I grinned.

"I think Gentry *thinks* he wants her," I murmured.

"He doesn't?" she asked. "You could've fooled me."

I nodded.

"She's good for him because he gives her treats." I shifted until I was facing her. Her eyes took me in as I gazed up at her. "But the moment she realizes that he's not going to give her goodies every single day, she'll go back to her asshole self."

Sway's brows rose.

"She's an asshole?" She had laughter in her voice. "Why is she an asshole?"

"She's spoiled rotten. Eats my shoes. Swims in the water and then tracks mud all over the house. Sometimes I find her in the weirdest places." I shook my head. "You have no idea of the weird places."

Sway's lips twitched.

"Like what?" she asked. "The bathtub?"

I laughed.

"No," I shook my head. "More like on top of the fridge. On top of the dining room table—which, as you can see, is bar height—and once I found her on my book shelf."

"What kind of dog is she?" She leaned her hip against the bed, and I moved my hand to cup the outside of her thigh.

"A Husky."

She grinned. "I always wanted a Husky. What does she look like?"

"Pure white." I smiled. "Although, I'm not sure she's completely one hundred percent Husky. The lady I got her from said that she was knocked up by one of her dogs. One was a Husky, and the other was a wolf hybrid mix."

Her mouth dropped open.

"You could have a wolf?" she gasped.

"Or, which is the more logical answer, she's a Husky," I pointed out. "She could go either way."

She pursed her lips.

"I'll let you know what I think when I see her again."

I patted her thigh, and my eyes closed involuntarily.

"Alright," she patted my hand and pulled away. "I'm going to go since your mom's here to take care of you now."

My eyes opened into slits.

"Don't you dare leave me here with them," I ordered.

She smiled at me, thinking I was joking.

I was far from joking, though.

"I can't handle them on the best of days when I'm at a hundred percent," I informed her sleepily. "When I'm sick like this, there's no way I can handle three of my brothers under my roof. Please save me from them."

She smiled at me like she thought I was joking, but I wasn't.

"Please," I pleaded.

"You're serious," she shook her head.

I nodded my head.

"I am." I nodded my head. "Come to bed."

"I can't sleep in here with you." She crossed her arms. "And all your other guest rooms are taken."

I patted the bed behind me again.

"Pleaseeee," I poked my lip out, putting a little bit extra whine in my pleading.

She sighed, long and loud, and I felt, more than saw, her move around the room.

My eyes were heavy, and it took everything I had not to give in to sleep.

"I don't have anything to wear," she said. "The only clothes I have in my car are too small. I've gained about twenty pounds in the last month."

"Good weight," I informed her. "You look edible."

She snorted. "I don't look edible," she sniffed. "I look fat."

I rolled over until I could see her staring at herself in my mirror above the dresser. "You're not fat. If you were fat, I'd tell you. And you, woman, are not fat. You're juicy and delectable. Not to mention every time I see your luscious ass in jeans I want to fuck it."

She lifted her nostrils in the cutest grimace I'd ever seen.

"I've never done that," she admitted.

"What?" I pushed. "Had anal sex…or had sex all together?"

Was that hopefulness I heard in my voice?

Hopefully she wouldn't hear that in my voice, because it made me sound like a caveman to want my woman virginal upon meeting her.

"Anal. But I can't say I'm a sexual connoisseur either." She admitted. "I haven't had any time. I've been working my ass off since I was eighteen to get where I am, and everyone in my family, except for my dad and brother, is in the medical field. There's no way I would randomly sleep with a stranger in this day and age. I met Langston, and we did give it a try, but…well…he was kind of sucky so we didn't do it more than twice before he'd decided I was no longer worthy of being his."

I tried to keep it cool, but I was unsure if my voice or face betrayed me.

"What does your dad do?" I asked as I grabbed for the covers and bunched them up over my hardening dick.

"He's a cop."

That did it.

My dick went down instantly.

"Bummer," I muttered. "You can wear one of my shirts."

I pointed to the dresser she was standing in front of and she grimaced again.

"They won't fit me," she hedged.

"Then sleep naked," I countered.

She glared.

Slipping the shirt off over my head—which proved to be a lot harder than normal—I bunched it up in my hands and launched it at her.

"Here," the t-shirt I'd been wearing had my jersey number on it, as well as the Lumberjacks' double L logo on the front breast area.

She immediately threw it back at me.

"No," she refused, shaking her head. "I'm not wearing that."

I frowned hard at her. "We just talked about this."

She smiled.

"It has nothing to do with my weight, and it not fitting," she told me. "And everything to do with the fact that I only wear the team shirts on game days."

My mouth dropped open.

"Are you saying that you have superstitions?"

She blinked.

"No."

I picked up the t-shirt.

"Then wear it."

She immediately shook her head.

"No!"

My mouth kicked into a small grin.

"Why won't you wear it?" I asked then.

"Because."

"Because why?"

"Because if I do, you might lose!"

I was laughing by this point.

"Half-Pint," I started. "That's called a superstition."

She glared and started rummaging through my drawers, coming up with one of my favorite shirts that I used to wear in high school. One that hadn't fit me in a very long time.

In fact, it was so small that I wasn't quite sure why the hell I even had it anymore.

With angry movements, she ripped her polo shirt off over her head, tossed it onto the chair in the corner of the room and snapped the shirt in the air to unfold it.

The moment she slipped it on, and the tight black Panthers baseball shirt slipped on over her breasts, I knew I'd made a good decision in saving it.

The t-shirt fit her like a glove.

Then she went and ruined me for all other women.

With a practiced move, she slipped her hand up the back of the shirt, unbuckled her bra, and slipped it off through one sleeve, followed shortly by the other.

My mouth went dry as I watched her breasts sway with the movement.

"Will you marry me?" I asked her.

She blinked.

"What did you just ask me?"

I licked my lips as she started to push her jeans down her thighs.

My cock started to pulse with each beat of my heart, and I wanted so badly for her to walk over here and sit on my cock.

I wanted to grab a hold of those luscious globes of her ass, dig my fingers in, and urge her to ride me hard.

"Black panties," I muttered. "I said I like your black panties."

She looked down at the black panties, and then back up to me.

"Huh," she said, then an evil grin lifted the corner of her mouth. "If you like the front," she turned. "Then you'll definitely like the back."

And oh, God, did I.

She was wearing those cheeky underwear where half of the ass cheeks hung out.

On others, they were definitely sexy.

On Sway…no words did her justice.

They were freakin' *amazing*.

I had a stern talking to with my cock while she was in the bathroom, and then switched off the light in anticipation.

The moment she got out and switched off the bathroom light, I was nearly on the verge of demanding she take me.

Begging wasn't beneath me.

But she crawled into bed moments after the light switched off, and then seconds later she was asleep.

How was that even possible?

She had to be faking. *Had to.*

But then a soft little snore had me blinking in surprise, and I laid there for another half an hour while I contemplated masturbating right next to her before I fell asleep.

***

"Ummm," my brother drawled as he held the paper up the next morning. "Is there something you'd like to tell us?"

I looked over at the paper, and my eyes widened.

Sway, who'd been behind me, was reading it and staring in horror.

"Why do they think we're getting married?" she cried. "Oh, my God. I need to call my parents!"

Then she left the room, leaving me to face my family. Alone.

"I wanted her in the room with me…so sue me."

CHAPTER 12

Even if the voices aren't real, they have some fucking awesome ideas!
-Hancock's secret thoughts

Hancock

"Parts," the reporter, the fifth in the last twenty minutes, grinned at me. "Gosh, but you're huge."

I nodded my head, aware that I would likely be on national television when I said what I had to say next, but I couldn't help it.

It was the perfect opener.

"That's what she said," I pointed to the person behind me.

I hadn't realized who it was until an outraged cry from Sway had me turning to look.

Then, like any man with a sense of humor, I burst out laughing and pissed her off even more.

By the time we ended the interview two minutes later—with me still laughing—I had tears running down my cheeks.

"That was wrong," Gentry chuckled. "But so good."

Sway glared hard, but I didn't miss the lip twitch that was trying to make itself known.

"I'm glad you're back, man," Gentry broke the tension.

My brows rose.

"Gentry," I looked at him fully. "I haven't missed any games."

He shrugged.

"But you missed all the practices," he said. "There've been two that I've had to go through without you."

I snorted. "That's why you should re-sign with the 'Jacks," I told him. "When your contract expires at the end of the season, you should remember the feeling you're having right now."

He rolled his eyes.

"My family's been bugging the shit out of me to come back to Oakland," he commented. "I told them I'd think about it if I got the offer from them."

I sighed.

"I already told you," I crossed my arms. "That you would hate living there. Think of all the snow."

"There's no snow in California, well, most of the state, anyway." Sway decided to drop her attitude and join in on the conversation.

I held my wrists out to her and she immediately started wrapping them without needing to be asked.

Gentry watched in amusement as I answered her silly comment.

"There's more possibility of snow there than there is here," I pointed out. "We only had one instance of snow last year, and that was one day and less than a quarter of an inch. Oakland got a foot last year."

Sway started to laugh.

"You're impossible," she informed me, patting my wrists. "You know they didn't get any snow." She paused before she got even a step away. "What's this?" she asked, touching my newest acquisition.

"A new glove I picked up from the equipment shed," I explained.

The equipment shed was more of a store of sorts. Sponsors donated items that they hoped we'd use, such as shoes, bats, balls, and tools of the trade.

"What are you doing to it?" She touched it.

I lifted the glove into my hand and unwound the five rubber bands I had holding the glove closed around the ball and showed her.

She frowned. "Why are you doing that?"

"You have to break a glove in. You can't just start using it during a game and expect it to perform to your liking," I told her. "So, you break it in, and this is one of the ways of doing it."

"What are the other ways?" she questioned.

"Some people beat it with a mallet to loosen up the leather," Gentry added in. "I used to drag mine behind my bike when I was younger."

"And you don't do that anymore?" Sway teased.

I shook my head.

"No," I disagreed. "The best way to break it in is to play with it. However, that ain't gonna happen during a game, and especially a game that's against the little fucker who tried to separate my head from my neck."

"He's not playing tonight," Sway said. "Or was I wrong about that?"

"You're not." I stood up and tucked my glove underneath my arm as I picked up my hat. "But that doesn't mean that the other players won't be on edge over what happened. They'll be waiting for me to try something…and, who knows? They might be right."

Sway sighed.

"I'll see you in a little bit," she smacked my ass lightly. "Now, get out of here. I have other players besides you to take care of."

My eyes widened, and a fierce sort of jealousy tore through me at the idea of her doing any other player than me.

Of course, I knew what she'd meant by the comment, but it didn't make it an easier pill to swallow as my mind chose that moment to race.

But then she had to go and ruin my anger by one simple comment that she tossed out offhandedly.

"Doesn't that beard bother you in the summer?" Sway asked, running a finger along the edge of my beard.

My brows rose. "Manliness isn't seasonal, Sway."

She tilted her head down and laughed, and I couldn't help but watch the way her breasts jiggled with each breath of laugher.

"Be good. You know where to find me before the game." She wiggled her eyebrows at me.

I snorted and smacked her ass, taking great joy in the resounding smack and the sting in my hand as I did it.

She squawked in outrage, and I tossed her a grin that couldn't be misinterpreted.

I wanted her.

I wanted her badly.

And I would have her.

By the end of the night.

She would be mine.

***

Was it possible to run the bases with a hard on?

Yes, yes it was.

But it was not easy to slide.

I stood up and dusted the dirt off my pants, glaring at the umpire.

"I was safe, and you damn well know it, Henderson!" I yelled. "You saw it, I saw it. Hell, even my eighty-year-old grandmother saw it from all the way up in the stands."

I gestured to the stands where my family was standing and yelling about the shitty call that was just made.

But that was just how the entire game went.

"You didn't touch second base," he said. "And Rhys touched it, meaning you're out."

"That's a load of bullshit and you know it!" I bellowed, anger making my voice shake with rage.

"Sorry, Parts. You know the drill." He gestured to the bench.

I crossed my arms over my chest.

"Coach is contesting it," I gestured with my chin. "I'll leave when you prove to me that I missed it."

I damn well hadn't missed it, and the ump needed to get his fuckin' eyes checked if he thought differently.

Henderson growled in frustration, and I caught the shake of his head before he turned and stomped up to the other umpires who were going over the call on the TV that was situated beside the home dugout.

My eyes automatically went to the dugout where Sway usually sat, but when my eyes finally trained on the spot, I realized it was empty.

Brows furrowing, I let my gaze wander and quickly realized why I'd been so pissed off in the first place.

She'd been chatty today.

Really chatty.

Like right now for instance.

She was chatting up Rhys like they were the very best of friends, and I found that I didn't like that anymore than when she was talking to Furious George the same freakin' way.

Jaw tightening, I turned my face away from the two and focused in on the umpires.

"You touched second," the third baseman for the other team, Milo something or other, said, breaking into my thoughts.

I turned my eyes only to take him in.

"I know," I mumbled.

"When I got into the draft, it was my dream to meet you one day," he informed me.

A grin broke out on my face as I realized I had a bona fide fan on my hands.

"Is that right?" I asked.

He nodded eagerly.

"Where'd you go to college?" I asked.

"Penn State," he answered quickly. "I was lucky to have a scout see me. If it wasn't for him, I wouldn't be here right now."

The kid was funny.

He also had one hell of a beard, which was abnormal for a kid his age.

"How old are you?" I asked, admiring his beard.

The kid brought his hand up to his beard and started to stroke it.

"How old do I look?" he challenged.

I snorted.

"Twenty-two, at most," I admitted. "The beard does things for you, though."

Milo started to chuckle.

"Thanks," he grinned. "And you're right. I'm twenty-two."

"You know anywhere good to eat?" I asked. "I'm going to force our athletic trainer to go out with me to dinner. You're welcome to come if you want."

He hesitated.

"I'm not sure if that's allowed…" he hesitated.

I shrugged. "Up to you, kid. Just throwing the offer out there."

He nodded, thinking.

"The Root is good," he finally decided. "It's got a good atmosphere, and not many people know about it. Locally owned and not many tourists go to it."

I nodded. "They have burgers?"

He nodded his head eagerly. "They do. The best."

The crowd started to boo, and I realized that the call had been handed out.

"They gave you the base," Milo muttered. "Knew they would."

I knew they would, too.

Henderson was a dick, and it seemed like he always made bad calls against me. Then again, when I was younger—about Milo's age—I decked him because he'd thought it'd be funny to laugh at something another player had said about my mother.

Granted, I wasn't the most chill of people when I was younger—and likely still wasn't if the rise of my blood pressure had anything to say about it—but that wasn't something you continued to hold over a person's head. I was ten years older now.

At thirty-two, I was nothing like the hotheaded boy who'd entered the league.

If anything, I was a hell of a lot more rounded and could control my temper just as well as the next guy.

"Fuckin' A," Milo muttered, then dove for the ball that I hadn't even realized had been hit.

"Shit!" I hissed, running for home.

The catcher got in my way at home plate, and I knew the ball was about to hit his glove any second.

And it did, landing right in the sweet spot.

With no other recourse, I slammed into the catcher like a linesman, hitting him so hard that my breath left me in a whoosh.

We both went down in a tangle of arms and limbs just like I'd done my last game.

Frantically, I tried to scramble for the base, which I somehow missed when I hit the catcher, and touched it.

That's when I saw the ball that was lying next to the plate.

"Fuck yes," I bellowed, getting to my feet.

I offered my hand down to the catcher, and he shook his head, refusing to take my hand.

Not caring, I pointed at Milo.

"You almost had me," I told him.

A grin kicked up the corner of his lips, but he didn't respond.

"Fucking bastard," the catcher mumbled as I walked away.

I chuckled as I walked back to the dugout, laughing when my teammates came out to meet me.

When I got to Rhys, I glared at him, and might have slammed chests with him harder than I needed to.

He gave me an annoyed look, but I knew he knew the reason for it.

I hadn't come out and said it in as many words, but he damn well knew she was mine.

I took a seat in my spot, and tried really hard not to glare at the woman who was sitting there reading a book like she didn't have a care in the world.

"What are you reading?" I grumbled.

She looked over at me for a few short seconds, and then turned back to her Kindle.

"A romance," she answered, not bothering to give me any more than that.

"What is it called?" I pushed.

"*Double Play.*"

"Hmm," I murmured. "What's it about?"

She gave me a narrow-eyed look.

"A baseball player and the greatest catch of his life," she answered. "Do you mind?"

I held my hands up in surrender and went back to watching the game.

We had this one in the bag.

We were ahead by ten, and we only had one inning left. Half if we managed to keep the lead.

Although it didn't happen often, it was possible that we'd get cocky and the other team might catch up.

Not today, though.

The players on the other team were playing like shit, which was what had gotten them in the hole in the first place.

The only way they'd win now was if we stopped trying, and that sure as fuck wasn't going to happen.

CHAPTER 13

I want someone to look at me the way I look at my Jeep.
-Sway's secret thoughts

Sway

I hesitated outside the exit to the parking lot, wondering whether I should wait for Hancock or not.

He hadn't said anything about wanting to do anything with me after the game.

I was also tired as hell from the plane ride, and the vehicle that was taking the athletic training staff was about to leave, so I made a choice and headed for the Jeep.

And, of course, Sinclair was driving.

Normally, I would've been in control of the rental, but since I rode in the day before with the team and the other staff who normally travel with the team, I didn't put my name on the rental policy.

Normally that wouldn't matter, but Sinclair was obviously smug about having the privilege of driving rather than being a passenger.

"Didn't think you were riding with us, Sway," Sinclair made a point to mention. "Did your *friend* give you the boot?"

I ignored him and walked to the back door, opened it, and took a seat next to Lacey.

"Hey, Lace," I smiled at her.

Lacey grinned and offered me a piece of gum, and I shook my head in the negative.

"No, thank you," I turned to look out the window.

"Everyone ready now?" Sinclair asked.

After three confirmations, one from Lacey, one from me, and one from our front seat passenger, John-John, aka JJ—our intern—we pulled out, heading straight for the hotel.

The hotel was less than five minutes away from the stadium, but after only two minutes of Sinclair's jerky driving, I realized that if I had to ride with him again, I'd very likely vomit.

When my head hit the window as he pulled in, I made an executive decision to talk to the team management. If a man wouldn't hesitate to do seventy in a forty, making me see my life flash before my eyes, he absolutely should not be driving the other members of the team's training staff while we were out of town.

Surely the management would want their staff to arrive to and from the games safely.

Right?

Lacey and I traded a few looks while JJ held onto the handle above his head like his life depended on it.

By the time we pulled under the covered awning, JJ looked deathly pale, Lacey was taking on a tinge of green, and I was wondering whether or not I could hack a walk back to the ballpark tomorrow.

It was only two miles.

If I left two hours early, surely I could make it on time.

"Thank for the ride," I muttered as I bailed out of the Jeep.

The Jeep itself was gorgeous. I'd always wanted a Jeep.

But I would prefer driving to riding in the passenger seat or the back seats.

"What's that face for?" Sinclair asked as he walked up beside me.

I didn't speak.

I could barely tolerate the man most of the time.

Between the car ride from hell with his reckless and erratic driving and his pungent cologne that smelled like a bundle of male magazines with a clashing variety of different sample scents inside, I was ready to bail.

Luckily, they'd sent my luggage up ahead of me, and I'd already checked into my room thanks to the hotel's app.

All I had to do was gather my key, and I was ready to go.

Lacey and JJ had done the same thing as me, while, unfortunately for him, Sinclair had not.

"Thank God," Lacey muttered under her breath as she stood next to me in line. "Freakin' gross."

JJ snorted. "This wasn't my first time riding with him. You'll be happy to know that he drove better than he usually does."

"Oh, God," I moaned. "If that was his 'good driving' I would hate to know what his 'bad driving' is like."

Lacey snorted.

"Can I help you all?" the man behind the desk asked with a brilliant smile on his face.

I gestured for Lacey and JJ to go first.

They both were quick and efficient, and they waved me off as they disappeared to the bank of elevators.

"We'll see you in the a.m." JJ called.

I waved them off and smiled.

Trying hard to produce a smile, I told the concierge my name, and he grinned widely at me before producing a blue key.

It was different than the ones JJ and Lacey had received, but I'd never thought to question it as I took it with a grateful nod before disappearing in the direction of the elevators.

After studying the number printed on the back of my key card, I yawned and leaned heavily against the gold embossed walls of the elevator.

My foot tapped silently to the beat of the classic rock pouring through the speakers, and I wondered idly if it was a new thing to not play elevator music in elevators any more.

Not that I was complaining. I found that I quite liked that it wasn't some boring instrumental tune. My eyes were already heavy. Not to mention I was riding to the floor below the top of the freakin' hotel.

Why I'd been put on the 14th floor, I didn't know, but I would take anything at this point.

After the last four days I'd had with Hancock—and how busy he'd kept me worrying about him—I was ready for a full night's sleep.

Anything would do at this point.

But what I walked into about two minutes later was quite a bit more than I'd expected.

"Whoa," I breathed. "This is freakin' amazing!"

The room was one large, open space like most hotel rooms, but it was plusher, decorated in rich reds and royal blues.

The far wall had one huge window that overlooked the lake that the hotel was situated in front of, and there was a large balcony beyond the window that I knew I'd be testing out later.

Maybe I'd even have my morning coffee on one of the lounge chairs.

The bed was also large. It was obviously a king-sized bed, but it looked almost bigger than normal due to the four, massive wooden posts on each corner, and the intricate carvings that adorned the head and footboards.

Then there were the many coordinating throw pillows on top of the bed that matched the comforter.

I ran my fingers over the bedding, surprised at how soft it was.

Was it real silk?

What the hell kind of place was this?

This wasn't a normal hotel room, that's for sure.

Knowing I needed a shower, I pushed away from the bed and headed for the bathroom, stopping once to confirm my hunch.

Opening one side of the closet, I breathed a sigh of relief when I saw my luggage where it belonged.

"Thank goodness," I groaned, closing the door and heading straight for the bathroom.

The bathroom...well, let's just say it wasn't your typical hotel bathroom. It had a fucking sauna in it.

And a tub that could double as a hot tub.

After taking care of a few necessities, I turned the huge shower on, exclaiming in excitement when I saw the multiple showerheads that were interspersed on the wall and ceiling of the enormous, walk-in shower.

"Come to mama," I moaned as I started to strip my clothes off.

I'd never, not once, stayed in a hotel like this.

I also knew which one I would be staying at next time I came into town.

"This place is awesome!" I cried as I tossed my clothes into the corner of the bathroom, then tugged my hair tie out of my hair, slinging it in the vicinity of the counter.

Which, I might add, had a freakin' fish tank built into the wall separating the his and hers sinks.

Well, for this stay they'd be mine and mine but that was cool!

I'd use both equally so neither one felt slighted.

Then I heard my phone ring.

After contemplating answering it for all of ten seconds, I decided that this shower was too important to pass up.

It was also my mother's ring tone, and I could call her back any time.

This shower, though, I'd only have for three days. So, I was going to make good use of it.

The moment I stepped inside a moan slid past my lips.

The water felt like it was hitting me everywhere at once.

My feet, my knees, the middle of my back, and my face.

Hell, there was even one aimed at my hooha—though it was a much gentler spray than the others.

The bathtub was even stocked with my favorite shampoo and conditioner, and not a tiny bottle of it, either. It was a massive bottle, one I'd buy at home and use over a month-long period.

The soap was also my brand, and a niggling feeling started to work its way into my brain before I cast it aside when I saw the instrument panel.

Another click on the control panel and all the showerheads started to pulse, even the one aimed at my pussy, causing my eyes to cross.

After twenty minutes of just standing there, I finally came to my senses and got to work cleaning my various body parts, saving my hair for last.

I'd just worked up a good lather of shampoo in my hair when I heard it.

"I had a feeling you would get here before me," the sound of a male voice broke into my shower.

I squealed and turned, soap running into my eyes as I opened them in the middle of my shampooing.

"What the hell, Hancock?" I cried, covering my breasts.

Or I tried to, at least.

My breasts were much too large to cover with just my hands.

I managed to shield my nipples from view and that was about it.

My pussy, luckily, got fully covered, but even that didn't feel like enough.

I was totally and completely naked in front of the hottest man in the world.

And he *was* the hottest man in the world. He'd won *Hour Magazine's*—one of the top celebrity magazines in the world—2017's Most Handsome Man Award.

Also, as a thank you to their readers, they'd printed a large poster in each magazine that featured Hancock's glowering face and nothing else.

I'd hung it on my bedroom wall next to my Fathead. There was no doubt in my mind that he'd seen that, too. The man missed nothing. I was sure, at this point, he was just being nice about my infatuation with him.

So yes, needless to say, I felt more than a little self-conscious standing there naked in front of him.

And then he started stripping.

"What are you doing?" I squeaked fearfully.

Hancock's beautiful eyes met mine as he stripped off his shirt.

"Joining you," he answered, not stopping his strip down.

When he got to his pants I turned around, closing my eyes and letting the water wash the shampoo away.

The moment I felt him behind me, my knees started to shake.

"You want to know why I want you so badly?" he asked conversationally.

"I don't know…" I cleared my throat. "Why?"

"You're beautiful." He let his finger trail up my right shoulder and then straight down my spine until it he came to a stop right above the top of my ass.

Goosebumps traced his path, and my nipples hardened.

"You take my breath away clothed," he murmured. "But without clothes?"

He pressed forward, and I nearly jumped two feet in the air when I felt his erection poke me in the ass.

"I'm a grown-ass man of thirty-two years, and if I wasn't sure it'd offend you, I'd come all over your ass right now with two strokes of my cock," he growled, pressing his lips against the back of my neck.

I licked my lips nervously.

"Who's to say that I'd be offended?"

The words came out of my mouth before I could stop them, and the breath left my lungs when he started to chuckle.

"I'm not saying that I don't want that—eventually—but right now?

Right now, I want to slide my cock into that pussy of yours and ride you until we both can't see straight," he admitted. "Badly."

I couldn't help but press back against him, and the resounding growl that left his lips had me clenching my thighs.

His hands went to my hips to still my jerky movements, and then left shortly after, one going up while the other went down.

Inadvertently, I sucked in as his hand trailed over my belly to the apex of my thighs, and he stopped only long enough to pinch my tummy.

"I love every fucking thing about you," he informed me. "Your stomach is perfect. Your hips are this beautiful hourglass shape that every woman in the world would kill for."

I'd never thought much about my actual shape.

In fact, I went out of my way *not* to think about it.

Sure, I was confident in my body. I knew that it'd never change unless I really did a drastic lifestyle change that included eating healthy, working out, and being smarter about my life decisions. So, I'd come to terms with who I was because one thing was for certain: I hated working out.

In fact, hate wasn't a strong enough word for it.

Loathe was more like it.

"You're thinking too hard," he punctuated that statement with a pinch of one nipple, and I gasped.

"So. We have two options here," he murmured, letting his lips trail against the curve of my neck.

"Yeah?" I asked.

"Yeah," he agreed.

"And what are those?" I licked my suddenly dry lips.

How that was even possible while I was in the freakin' shower, I didn't know, but they were.

"One, we could dry off, go lay on the bed and watch TV," he started.

My belly twisted.

That wasn't what I wanted.

Not at all.

Not even a little bit.

"What's the second option?" I asked breathlessly.

"Option two is I fuck you until the wee hours of the morning, and we only stop when the sun starts to kiss the sky," he growled low and deep.

I groaned when his hand started to tangle in the curls between my legs. His forefinger and thumb came together to pinch my clit, and my entire lower half shrank back in reaction, causing pain mixed with a little bit of pleasure to burst through me.

"You have a baseball game tomorrow night," I pointed out. "And I have to be at the field about an hour before that. Staying up all night to do what you just…suggested…isn't such a good idea."

It killed me to say it, but someone had to be logical here.

"So, you don't want to do this?" he asked carefully.

I turned in his arms, and he let me. His eyes trained straight on mine as I situated myself in his arms.

"I've never wanted anyone or anything so badly in my life…" I informed him. "But I don't want to be responsible for screwing up your rest schedule before tomorrow's game."

His lips quirked, and my hands lifted involuntarily to run over his beard.

He turned his face into my hand, and I started to scratch his beard with my nails as he watched me.

"You want me?"

In answer, I swallowed my fear and leaned forward.

My breasts pressed into his overheated skin, pushing against the rock-hard ridges of muscle also known as his abs.

My hands went to his shoulders, and I leaned up onto my tippy toes, pressing my lips against his.

His beard tickled my lips and cheeks, but that didn't take away from the excitement that coursed through me when our lips connected.

It was the first time I'd been the one to initiate anything between us, and I found that I quite liked how powerful it made me feel.

I felt on top of the freakin world when he groaned in defeat, his mouth coming down onto mine, his head slanting as his tongue plunged between my lips, urgently taking over the kiss.

When my back hit the cool tile wall, I tightened my hands, which inevitably caused my nails to dig in to the sensitive skin of his back.

"We're about to take this relationship to the next level, darlin', from something innocent to something that's anything but innocent," he murmured, pulling back slightly so his lips were only inches from my own.

I studied his eyes in the harsh light hanging over the top of the shower, knowing that whatever we did tonight meant more to me than just a casual fuck.

And I wasn't the type of person who entered into relationships lightly.

I'd learned the hard way that having different expectations about things lead to problems, and if I was being honest, I really liked Hancock. I didn't want anything bad to happen between us. I was beginning to really like him, and if this didn't work out between us, then not only would our work life be complicated, but I'd lose a man who I was quickly counting as one of my closest friends.

And I didn't have many of those.

It would hurt me deeply not to have him there any longer.

It'd only been two weeks.

Fourteen days.

Three hundred and thirty-six hours.

In the grand scheme of things, that didn't seem all that long.

Not to most people, anyway.

To me, though…well, that was a long time.

I may not have had many people that I counted as close friends, but the ones whom I did have were because we'd formed those relationships and bonds quickly. Something that my mom has said was one of my greatest flaws.

Which was probably why I dated the men I'd dated in the past.

Hancock was different, though. I knew, instinctively, that he was going to change my life. The moment I walked into the dugout and sat in his spot—*on purpose*—I knew my life was about to become very different.

And I'd been right.

"You have to promise me something," I loosened my hold on him. "If this goes bad…we have to promise to work things out. To make it so that we can co-exist and still do our jobs without anything coming between us."

His mouth kicked up in the grin.

"You're saying that after I fuck you—if we decide to call it quits—that I'll have to act like I haven't been inside of you?" he teased.

I slapped his arm, the wet sound of our skin connecting echoing off the tile, sounding like I'd hit him a lot harder than I actually had.

His mouth quirked up in a small grin, and I soothed the hurt I'd just inflicted by running my hand over the bulging skin of his bicep.

"Be serious," I ordered.

His face sobered.

"Let me tell you something, Sway." He pressed me backward until he was completely covering me, his large frame towering over me like an avenging angel. "I'll do just about anything to make you happy. That means, should things go bad between us, I'll do whatever I have to do to make sure you're comfortable. If I have to fucking leave the Lumberjacks to do that, I will. I'll do that because I want you to be happy. I'll do just about anything to see a smile light up your face, even if it's because I'm leaving that you do it."

My eyes closed of their own volition, and when I opened them again after I'd regained my composure, I ordered my brain to take a hike and let my heart make all the decisions.

"Yes."

"Yes?" he confirmed.

I nodded.

His grin would've lit up the bathroom if it were possible, and I had to clench my legs together to ease the ache that that smile caused.

"So…" he pressed his lips against the corner of my collar bone. "Have you ever had shower sex?"

"I'm clean as a whistle," I blurted. "I had to pass a full physical to start my job with the Lumberjacks."

My word vomit caused him to smile, and I narrowed my eyes.

"Well?" I asked when he got finished laughing quietly at me.

"I'm clean. I haven't had sex since…before you." He growled. "And I passed a full physical myself." He cleared his throat. "Did you tell me this for the reason I think you told me this?"

"I have the birth control implant right here," I pointed to the soft skin underneath my arm, and his eyes automatically went to the place on my arm where I was indicating.

"That looks painful," he muttered, taking in the raised skin.

"It wasn't too bad," I admitted.

How was he able to have a normal conversation right now? With his large dick sandwiched between both of our bodies? With the way my nipples were pebbled against his big, defined, hairy chest.

My hand moved up to swirl the soft hair around his nipples, and he growled low in his throat.

"Don't," he ordered.

My brows rose as my eyes moved to his.

"Why not?" I inquired.

"Because I'm barely hanging on here," he admitted. "You start touching me, and I'll start forgetting that I'm trying to be a gentleman."

My mouth kicked up at the corners as a grin split my face.

I never thought of myself as sexy, but in this man's arms, I felt all kinds of beautiful.

The way he looked at me, the way his big body towered over mine.

I'd never in my life felt petite before, but in Hancock's arms, I felt downright small.

"You're thinking too hard," he murmured, making some decision. "Stop thinking so hard."

"I can't help it," I told him honestly. "I…"

He shut me up with his mouth, slamming his down onto mine as he curled one large arm around my waist and pulled me in tight to him.

When he was sure he had a good grip on me, he moved, maneuvering us until I was in front of the large seat that took up the back half of the shower, and then twisted so I was facing it.

Then, without another word, he shoved me forward, making sure to hold onto my hips as he did.

I gasped as I instinctively bent over, my hands going to the tile bench as I looked back at him over my shoulder.

"I want to slam inside of you," he rasped. "I want to line up with your tight hole, force my way inside and watch as you take me."

I blinked.

"And, why can't you?" I pushed him.

That's when I felt his cock up at my entrance starting to press inside.

My mouth opened wide the head of his cock started to stretch me.

I'd, of course, known he was big.

I'd seen him in boxers. I'd seen him through the jetted waters of the whirlpool. I'd felt him against me. But I'd never really looked at him.

But it was another thing all together to experience it—to have him pushing inside of me.

The man was massive.

Positively huge.

I was one hundred percent sure that he wasn't going to fit, and I knew exactly why he said what he said only moments before.

He literally couldn't.

Could he?

Then he started to slip inside me further, and my eyes widened in surprise, with a little bit of discomfort.

"You make me forget," he started to pull backwards.

But then I pressed against him, letting him know, in no uncertain terms, that I wanted him to continue.

I wanted to know if I would be able to take all of him. *I had to know.*

I had a feeling that this was something he'd always wanted to do and couldn't. I wanted to be different.

I wanted to give him something that no one else had ever been able to give him.

Hancock struck me as a man who could go all night long.

A man who would make me feel things that I'd never felt before.

And I wanted to do the same for him.

If that was taking me like he wanted to take me, then I'd give him that.

Every damn time and twice on Sunday.

Sensing my need to please, he started to press forward again, his large cock filling me up so fully that I was panting by the time his hips met my round bottom.

"Oh, God," he grated. "This is the best fucking feeling in the world."

"Being inside of me?" I panted, my eyes nearly crossed from how full I felt.

"Yes," he whispered. "So tight and wet. I've never felt anything like this before in my life."

I'd never felt it before either. Then again, I'd never once felt anything like this because I'd never had a man inside of me bare. Nor had I ever had sex in the shower. And now that I was thinking about it…there wasn't much I could say about my limited sexual experience.

Hancock was literally shattering all kinds of records right now.

And adding to that list was the near spontaneous orgasm I was on the brink of.

I'd thought orgasms were a myth—at least the ones from vaginal penetration. The man hadn't even done much more than stick his large dick inside of me, and I was practically on the verge of coming.

That had to be some kind of record.

Then he started to move, and I forgot my own name.

My hands on the lip of the seat tightened, and I spread my legs wider to accommodate his hips.

The moment my feet moved, the angle he was entering me changed, and I immediately went from being on the brink of an orgasm to having one.

The blunt head of his cock hit some magical place so deep inside of me that a silent scream left my lips.

My breasts began to sway with his movements, and as he felt my orgasm taking hold, he pounded into me faster and harder. My legs started to burn with the effort it took to hold myself up against his thrusts.

"Oh, God!" I cried out loudly, the scream echoing off the walls, mixing with the wet slap of skin meeting skin.

His grip on my hips tightened as my pussy clamped down so hard on his cock that there was no way he could mistake my release for anything other than what it was.

"Oh, fuck," he groaned tightly as his thrusting became erratic.

My eyes closed and I did nothing else but feel as the most blissful feeling in the world took me over.

Somewhere in the back of my mind, I was aware that he was coming, too. My mind, however, was so focused on my own pleasure that I had nothing left in me to pay attention to his.

By the time I came back to myself, Hancock was curved over the length of my back, one arm looped under my breasts while the other was planted on the bench and supporting our weight.

Both of us were breathing so hard that it was more than obvious that we were both shaken by what had just transpired.

"I had no idea that sex was like that," I admitted breathlessly.

"It's not, *normally*," he admitted just as breathlessly. "I haven't lost my breath like that since I was fifteen years old."

"You had sex when you were fifteen years old?" I squeaked, incredulity filling my voice.

"Yep," he murmured. "I was a lively, growing boy. That, and I was a baseball player with a goatee. I was pretty damn irresistible."

My answering snort was what he was looking for, and he pulled out of me carefully before he let me loose, his hands, now gentle on my hips, steadying me.

"You okay?" he asked, pressing a bearded kiss to the top of my shoulder as I stood.

I nodded.

Fan-fucking-tastic was more like it, but I didn't tell him that, his ego would be just fine without that little boost.

Instead, I settled on something that was more subdued but definitely got the point across.

"Better than okay."

He hummed in happiness as he grabbed the bar of soap from the soap dish before he quickly rubbed it over his body and then got to work on mine.

"You're responsible for this, aren't you?" I asked, gesturing to my shampoo and body wash.

His grin was almost boyish as he turned the shower off once he'd deigned I was clean. He took extra special care of my breasts and between my thighs, which inevitably made me ready to go all over again.

He was all business, though, as he stepped out of the shower and grabbed two towels. He handed one over to me and wrapped the second one around his trim waist. I began to absently towel myself off while my eyes took in his perfectly chiseled frame as water droplets rolled down his tight abs, disappearing into the top of the towel.

CHAPTER 14

If my dog could talk, I'd have no reason to talk to people.
-Hancock's secret thoughts

Sway

"You're about to get bent over again." Hancock's rumbly voice broke into my perusal.

I blinked, looking up at him as innocently as I could which caused him to laugh.

"I saw you," he informed me. "And in about ten minutes, I'll be more than up for whatever you're willing to do to me."

"Me do to you?" I asked in alarm, tugging the towel around my breasts.

He wouldn't want me to be on top, would he? Because that would definitely not be cool.

The one and only time I was ever on top was, of course, with Langston.

After he complained about my ass pushing his legs uncomfortably into the bed, I'd climbed off, refusing to get on top again.

Then Langston had to go and mention how my breasts jiggled and my belly squished together.

Normally—if I was standing—my belly tended to be fairly flat. But bending over causes almost everyone to have belly rolls, and I wasn't an exclusion.

It was apparently a big turn off for Langston because he never tried to have sex with me in that position again.

Then again, the position itself hadn't felt all that good, so there was really nothing to complain about. Langston's cock had been about five inches, fully erect, and even with me on top, I couldn't feel him like I was thinking I should be able to.

Hancock, though…well, let's just say he would probably rip me a new one if I was on top. But the sheer size of his cock was likely going to make that position difficult.

"What are you thinking about?" Hancock questioned as I followed him out of the bathroom, my mind still swirling with the possibility that he wanted to ask me to be on top.

He walked straight over to the large bed dominating the big, open room and started to push pillows off.

Thankful for the change in subject he'd inadvertently offered me, I pounced on it.

"What are you doing?" I asked as I watched him tug the comforter down on the bed.

It landed on the floor in a large heap, and I frowned.

"I read online that hotels don't wash their comforters, and ever since then I've yanked them off and only slept with the sheets."

I blinked in surprise.

"Why would they not wash the comforter?" I grimaced, thinking about how revolting it would be if that were true. "That's disgusting."

He nodded his head and started to rip the corner of the sheet off the bed.

"It is," he agreed as he bent over to peer at the mattress itself.

"Now what are you doing?" I pushed.

"Looking for a bed bug infestation," he mentioned almost casually. "It looks good to me."

"What?" I cried. "Bugs?"

His lips twitched.

"I wasn't saying there would actually be any here, but it's also something I always check for, just in case," he admitted sheepishly.

"Another superstition?" I asked casually, walking to my suitcase and pulling it carefully out of the closet.

The moment I moved mine I saw his, and my mouth twitched.

I couldn't figure out how I'd missed it.

It was bright freakin' red.

But it was smaller than mine and it'd been directly behind mine, so that likely accounted for why it was overlooked.

Once I had it next to the counter, I dumped it over on its side and squatted down to open it.

The move made the towel ride up, exposing my pussy to the floor, but I ignored it, instead looking for a bra to contain my massive DDs.

I wish they had squats for boobs.

The moment I found my bra, I stood up and let the towel drop, completely unaware that I had an audience that was avidly watching my every move.

Once my bra—a prettier one than normal since I knew I'd be seeing Hancock this weekend—was hooked, I pulled the cups up over my breasts and then worked my hands into the straps and situated it.

Then resituated it since my breasts were so unruly.

Then again, this bra was notorious for pushing my cleavage up instead of actually of doing anything to contain it.

There was a rule about bras for bustier ladies. *A bra couldn't be pretty and be comfortable.* That was just the cold, hard truth.

It sucked, but we ladies learned to live with it.

After deciding that the bra was just going to have to do since I hadn't packed any more, I grabbed a black lace pair of underwear, bent slightly over the bed with my hand touching the top to steady myself, and lifted a leg.

And that's when I heard the groan.

I froze and dropped my leg, turning slightly to where I'd heard the groan originate from, and blinked when I saw Hancock sitting on what looked to be a dressing chair directly behind me. He was staring at my ass like he wanted to devour it, and I made a grab for the towel.

"Don't," he ordered harshly, then lightened his tone. "Please don't."

I froze with my hand around the towel, and knew that I had a decision to make. I could either continue to be self-conscious around him, or let it happen naturally. He'd made no bones about the fact that he liked my body. He liked that I was on the thicker side.

Hell, if the erection that was tenting the towel, which might I add was wrapped fairly tightly around his waist since it was pinned with the way he was sitting, was anything to go by, then he quite obviously liked what he saw.

And I knew, *I knew*, that I was going to give *me* to him.

All of me. The good and the bad.

I was going to be me. I wasn't going to be a fraction of me like I was with Langston.

I was going to let him see that I enjoyed food. I was going to let him see that when I came home from work, my bra came off because wearing bras sucked. I was going to show him everything, and hope that he was there when the dust settled around me.

Once the decision was made, I dropped the towel, and then turned to sit on the bed directly in front of him.

His mouth was relaxed, but his eyes were dancing with happiness.

"You made a good decision, Half-Pint," he informed me. "I'm glad."

I could feel the flush taking over my face.

"Want to play a game?" he asked casually.

My head tilted to the side, and I stared at him.

"What kind of game?" I finally worked up the courage to ask.

The smile that overtook his face was as close to a leer as I would say one could get.

"One that ends in your orgasm and mine," he promptly replied. "So, what do you say?"

"What does this game entail?" I pushed as if his erection hadn't jumped in anticipation, and his pebbled nipples weren't affecting me at all.

"It entails you doing what I say, when I say it, and you get rewarded," he explained teasingly.

Before, I hadn't doubted that Hancock was an alpha male, but now...well, now I knew he was. He was an alpha in the bedroom and out. There was no doubting it now.

The fact might've been a turnoff for anyone else. Generally, I made it a rule to stay away from the bossy men since I had enough of bossy men growing up.

I liked to do my own thing, and I enjoyed it.

Being bossed around wasn't my idea of a good time, and if someone tried, I'd let them know really quick that it wasn't for me.

But when Hancock did it, I lost the ability to think.

The actual rules didn't matter. If he wanted me to do it, I'd do it, and all he had to do was ask…or tell.

If he said jump, I'd ask how high.

"Okay," I said without hesitation. "What's in it for me?"

The teasing didn't have the desired effect.

The moment I agreed, he was out of his chair and pushing me backwards onto the bed, his large hand between my legs.

In a matter of seconds, he was playing with my clit, swirling it around with his thumb while his fingers probed my wetness.

Which was embarrassing.

We'd been out of the shower a whole five minutes and my readiness for him was more than evident.

Something he found himself liking.

Immensely.

His mouth came down on mine as the first finger penetrated my depths, not stopping until he was at the webbing of his fingers.

"So fucking wet," he said in between breaths against my lips.

I moaned shakily as I moved my heels up to rest on the edge of the bed, and he moved the rest of the way in between them.

The towel he still had around his hips rasped against the inside of my thighs, but the things he was doing to my clit and pussy had me forgetting everything else that had happened.

"Please," I pleaded. "Please."

I was going to come.

He'd only thrust one strong finger into my pussy and had played with my clit for less than thirty seconds, and I was already *right there*.

The moment I realized I was close, I came.

Just giving it the awareness that it needed was enough to draw a scream from my lungs as another orgasm, my second in under thirty minutes, overtook me.

My pussy rippled around his long finger, and being the expert he was, he stopped the movement on my clit, knowing on instinct that I would be too sensitive for his continued ministrations.

It was only after I caught my breath that he spoke his next words.

"That's what's in it for you," he growled against my lips. "So, are you ready to play?"

God yes, I was ready to play.

All freakin' night long if he wanted me to.

"Yes."

Was there any other answer that I could give at this point?

The sane answer was: hell no.

***

Hancock

"Come to the balcony with me," I ordered, holding out my hand for her. "And lose the bra."

She looked down at the bra, then looked at my hand.

Taking it, I helped her stand and let it go as she deftly unhooked the bra that she'd just put on.

The moment her breasts were free again, my hard cock became harder.

God, she was magnificent.

Her porcelain white skin was milky and smooth. Then there were her pretty pink nipples.

Though they were on the larger side, I found them to be freakin' perfect.

I couldn't wait to see how much of those pretty nipples I could fit into my mouth.

And God, her pussy was addictive.

Waiting for her to look into my eyes, I brought up the finger that'd only moments before been inside of her, and sucked the juices off in one long lick.

Her eyes widened, and that beautiful blush that she'd had all night came back out to play.

"You're crazy," she whispered.

I grinned, letting her know I took no offense to that title and held out my hand once again.

"Come 'ere," I ordered.

She easily put her hand inside mine, and I walked with her to the balcony doors.

Once we were standing directly in front of them, I reached to the side and hit the lights, plunging the room into darkness.

"I had some wine brought out here for you," I told her.

"What about you?" she asked causally.

"No wine for me. Not before tomorrow's game," I admitted.

Though, I likely wouldn't have had any with her anyway. I was more of a beer guy than a wine guy.

Sway hummed in understanding and pushed the large glass sliding door open.

It rolled almost silently as she pushed, and then I followed her outside, my feet just as bare and quiet as hers as we made our way across the tiled balcony.

"This place is amazing," Sway gasped as she took in the view of the river down below.

It was. Every time we came to this city, I stayed in this hotel just because of the view.

The team had stayed here when I was a rookie, and then they'd changed venues the next couple of times.

The coaches forced the entire team to stay in the same place, and that was fine…if they were staying in a place I wanted to stay. Lucky for me they picked the good venue in this particular city, so I didn't have to act like I stayed at one hotel when I really stayed at another.

"Are we on the top floor?" she asked absently as she looked over the balcony.

The sight she made, made my breath catch, and I had to resist the urge to walk up behind her, bend my knees, and sink inside of her.

Though she'd probably enjoy it—and I knew for sure *I* would enjoy it—I chose to have a conversation with her first before I took her again.

We needed to be on the same page before we went any further.

"We're two floors below the top," I told her. "The top floors are penthouses that the owners live in."

"Ahh," she nodded her head in understanding. "I'd live here too, if I could. This place puts mine to shame."

"Your place isn't that bad," I noted.

She smiled at me over her shoulder.

"It used to be my grandmother's," she explained, turning around.

My breath hitched in my throat at her beauty.

Standing there, the concrete wall of the balcony at her back, her chest jutted forward as she leaned her elbows against the top of the railing, and her hair moved all around her, swaying in the soft breeze that came off the river.

I could barely make out her creamy white breasts, and everything else was cast in shadows as the darkness surrounded us.

"I bought my house from an old man," I shifted in my seat, glad that I still had my towel. "He reminded me of my grandfather."

If my cock was out in the open and free to do what it wanted, then it'd likely have her attention focused on it. Instead, her eyes were on my face, but had it been uncovered, she wouldn't have been able to stop herself from looking.

"I didn't buy mine," she grimaced. "My grandmother is renting it out to me until she decides what she wants to do with it. She had a fall a few weeks ago, and she and my family decided that it was in her best interest to be under supervision while she recovered."

My brows rose.

"She's in there for good," she answered my silent question. "She thinks it's only temporary, but it's not. She broke her hip—but a retirement home that can manage her meds and keep an eye on her at this point is best, and even she knows it. She was having trouble before she was injured. I'd offered to help, but I travel too much with the team, as does my brother, but with his team. Though, she'd never admit that she's in need of help. This way she saves face."

I nodded in understanding, then picked up the bottle of wine that was sitting next to the chair and tugged the cork out of the top.

I'd opened it while Sway had been in the shower and had set this all up intending to woo her into bending to my will, but she'd willingly taken me into her body without even the slightest bit of cajoling. Not that I would complain about that. The woman could do no wrong in my eyes.

"What are you thinking so hard about over there?" she interrupted my thoughts.

I poured her a glass of wine and reached across the small space that separated us. "Thinking about how perfect you are."

"You don't know me well enough to say I'm perfect yet," she informed me. "I'm about as far away from perfect as one can get."

I shrugged.

"You'll have to prove that to me over time, I suppose." I amended. "Right now, with you standing here like that in front of me, you look pretty damn perfect to me."

A small ghost of a smile graced her lips before she took a sip of the wine

"This is good." She looked at the glass. "What kind is it?"

I held up the bottle.

"Got it at the grocery store. Fourteen dollars. I have no fuckin' clue about wine. I picked one up that I saw a few other ladies get," I explained.

She started to laugh.

"I like how you think. Normally, I drink from the box," she admitted, as if she was letting me in on a secret.

I patted the outdoor couch seat beside me, and she pushed off the wall, her breasts bouncing with the movement, and started toward me.

I watched the sway of her breasts, and I nearly groaned when she bent down and put her hand into the seat before planting that delectable ass on the cushion beside me.

She wasn't touching me, but she was so close to me that I could feel the heat of her due to her closeness.

She sat partially sideways, allowing her arm to rest on the back of the cushion we were sitting on.

I'd also thought ahead, placing a couple of towels on the couch so nothing belonging to our bodies was actually touching the seats.

Which was good, seeing as we would both be naked on it very, *very* soon if our breathing was anything to go by.

"I can't believe you play well in weather like this. It's like being back home, only about ten degrees hotter," she murmured.

"Arizona has more of a dry heat than we do. Where we have a humid heat, they have just heat. More of it, yes, but not completely worse than what we suffer through. At least I can breathe," I told her. "Sometimes at home, when I have the mask on, it feels like I can't get a complete breath when it comes to the humidity."

She took one last sip of her wine and leaned over me, placing the drink on the very edge of the table.

Although likely innocent, my entire body went on alert the moment the tip of her nipple brushed against my chest.

My whole body felt like a lightning bolt shot through it, and I nearly lost my composure and dragged her from her position to bury my face between her breasts.

Somehow, though, I managed to sit completely still, allowing her to return to her seat without making an ass of myself.

"I have a confession," she blurted, her face turning down and away from mine.

My lips kicked up.

Though I couldn't see the blush, I knew it was there.

She had me intrigued. What did she have to confess that she was embarrassed about?

"What's that?" I questioned, turning in the seat so my back was against the arm of the couch. My leg pulled up to rest against the couch cushions, which inevitably made my cock jut forward, tenting the towel.

Not that she could see that my cock was now pointing directly at her. It was too dark.

I knew, though.

Then it started to bounce, and I almost interrupted what she was about to say by pulling her into my arms. However, the next words out of her mouth had me freezing.

"I know all your stats," she blurted.

My brows rose.

"Yeah?" I asked.

I knew this already.

I'd seen her wall. I'd seen my life-size picture. It honestly didn't surprise me at this point, and I kind of liked that she was a tad bit obsessed with me.

She nodded.

"And I followed your career, starting from when you were in college." The moonlight lit half of her face, enabling me to see the sheepishness that was written all over it.

"You haven't mentioned that before," I teased.

"I had a major crush on you," she huffed out a small laugh. "It was embarrassing, really. That first day, when you said to move out of your seat...that was the highlight of my life, having you talk to me."

I snorted.

"I'm no different or better than the next man, Sway," I groaned. "Don't put me on a pedestal because I'll surely fall," I hesitated. "I'm just a country boy. I grew up in Arkansas, on a farm. I used to get up at the crack of dawn, check the cows. Run fences. Hell, three quarters of the time I went to school with cow shit on my shoes."

She started to giggle. "Like your father?"

I nodded in all seriousness. "Exactly like my father. When I'm done with baseball, that's where I'm going to be. Right back there, hand in hand with my brothers, taking care of the ranch."

"You're not going to live fat and happy on the lake?" she giggled.

I grinned. "Well," I hesitated, just now thinking about having to leave the lake house behind. "The fat part, no. I don't want to be fat. But I'll keep my lake house. I love the fuck out of it."

She snorted.

"So eloquent," she teased.

"That's me, never at a loss for words, even if they aren't so well spoken," I rolled my eyes, and we sat in silence as we both thought about what I'd said.

"How far away is your parents' ranch?" she asked, interrupting my silence.

"They live just over the Texas/Arkansas border. They own about 200 acres, and run some wild horses, as well as cows, on it," I expounded.

"My family and I grew up in the city. I have never once ridden a horse," she smiled. "Though, my mom says I rode a donkey once."

I chuckled. "That's brave of you. All the donkeys I've come into contact with are ornery. I don't think I would ever try to ride one."

"It was once at a fair," she explained, her hand dropping down to the seat between us. Only inches from my still hard cock.

If she lifted her hand slightly up and to the right, she'd be touching it, and my dick pulsed at the thought.

"I was a newborn when I was on my first horse with my dad. He said it was the only way to get me to shut up…apparently, I had colic like a motherfucker for three months," I explained.

She shivered. "I can't imagine. My brother has a kid, you know."

My brows rose.

"What?" I asked. "Isn't he like twenty-two?"

She nodded. "He is. Though, he got his high school girlfriend pregnant when she was sixteen, and he was seventeen."

I blinked.

"Are they still together?" I asked.

She nodded her head. "They are."

"Wow," I murmured. "You think they'll make it?"

A small grin graced her mouth.

"I do," she confirmed with a short tilt of her head. "They have that once-in-a-lifetime kind of love that will stand the test of time."

"Fame changes people," I muttered.

She nodded her head in agreement. "That's why he went to the team he did. It was close to us, and he had our parents support, as well as her parents, if they ever needed it."

"That's amazing," I murmured. "My older brothers have been married since they were all eighteen."

"They're married?" Sway asked in surprise.

I nodded.

"They all have three kids, too," I confirmed. "Hannibal and I are the lone rangers."

She snickered.

"They don't seem the type," she admitted. "Too much wildness, I guess."

"They're wild," I agreed. "Dad and Mom raised a bunch of hotheads."

"Why weren't you married at eighteen, then?" She tilted her head to the side.

"I almost was," I said. "But when I went to college, she didn't want to go with me. She wanted to stay there and play the rancher's wife…and that just wasn't what I was looking for at that point in time."

"So, you broke up?" she guessed.

I nodded. "Ellie and I were good together…but she was too meek. I should've seen that for what it was."

"You're not telling me all of it," Sway guessed.

I tossed her a grin, despite the fact that she couldn't see it.

"No, I'm not," I agreed. "But I don't want you to think badly of my brother before you've had the chance to meet him."

"Okay," Sway hesitated. "Tell me."

I sighed.

"When I left, Hannibal…"

"I still can't get over his name." Sway interjected.

I nodded.

She waved me on to finish, even though I knew she wanted to say something else about, it which was a fairly normal reaction to Han's name. Now, it worked since he was a special operations bad ass. Then, when we were in school, everyone teased him relentlessly.

Though that was the name of the game in school. You were made fun of for just about anything, names included.

"Hannibal had about three weeks before he went into the Air Force after I left, and in that time, they got close."

"You mean they did it," Sway demanded, sounding offended on my behalf.

I started to chuckle.

"Down tiger," I soothed, patting her bared thigh.

"I can't help it," she grumbled. "I don't think it's right. Especially after only a couple of weeks since you split."

"You have to understand," I murmured. "In high school, Hannibal, Ellie, and I were a package deal. Where I went, they went. We were The Three Musketeers, and we did everything together."

"That's still not right." She crossed her arms over her chest.

"No, maybe not," I agreed. "But I didn't do anything with Ellie, thankfully. She was never really mine," I hesitated. "I never made her mine…do you understand?"

"You never made her yours," she nodded her head. "Meaning you never fucked her."

I nodded in agreement. "Right. I'm not proud of how I acted when I was younger, and maybe that's why I acted the way I did, because I knew she wasn't mine."

"And your brother somehow did before he left and then felt obligated to marry her?" Sway guessed.

I grinned.

"My brother felt like shit…and still does. However, they're not married." I pointed out. "So don't make him feel like it when you meet him. He's a sensitive soul…once you get past the crusty exterior."

"Are your brother and Ellie still together?" Sway asked.

I shook my head.

"They aren't," I grimaced. "After he left, he never came back. I think they still talk, but she wants to have the whole marriage, five point seven kids, and matching male and female Golden Retrievers. That's never been his dream. They tried to give it a go, but the first time he wasn't able to talk for six weeks, she called it off."

"Five point seven kids?" she grinned, then shook her head, catching my teasing despite the tense conversation. "I couldn't even imagine. If you were in the military, I might seriously be rethinking our relationship right now. The idea of anyone I care about putting their life on the line on a daily basis scares the absolute crap out of me."

She lifted her hand that was resting between us up, and that's when she touched my cock, halting all conversation.

I hissed when she came into contact with it, but I managed to hold onto my composure. *Barely.*

At least until she latched onto it with her hot little hand, rendering me unable to think clearly.

The next thing I knew, I had a lap full of willing woman, and I didn't have one single thing to complain about.

"You wanna know something?" she breathed, her mouth only millimeters away from mine.

"What?" I growled, leaning forward a fraction of an inch until our lips were just barely touching.

She didn't kiss me, and I didn't kiss her.

Instead, I waited to see what she had to say, and she didn't disappoint.

"I'd wait for you forever," she whispered. "If you left, I'd be here, right where you left me, waiting for you to come back. Even if it killed me to do that."

A smile kicked up the corner of my lips.

"Is that right?" I teased, latching onto her hips and pushing her down as I ground my hips up.

She gasped when the hard column of my cock came into contact with her pussy. Even covered with a thick towel it knew exactly where it wanted to go.

"Take this off," she tugged on the towel.

She stood up when I couldn't budge it between us, and I momentarily lost my train of thought when her pussy came to within a few inches of my face.

"Oh, God," she inhaled, trying to insert some space between us, while I was wrapping my arms around her.

My hands at the backs of her thighs wouldn't let her.

My first reaction to being so close to her was to inhale her scent. My nose traced down her abdomen, inhaling lightly.

There was a faint trace of the soap I'd used to wash her a few minutes before, but mostly it was just her mouthwatering aroma. All *fucking* her.

Stiffening my tongue, I found the top of her slit and pushed, letting my tongue slide down between the cleft.

"Sweet baby Jesus," she whispered, her hands in my hair tightened to the point of pain.

I couldn't reach much with the way she was standing, thighs slightly apart, but I could reach her clit.

I lowered my mouth and my tongue darted out to play with it, swirling around the tight bud while she squirmed against my face.

"Fuck!" she cried out. "Hancock! I'm close."

I smiled against her mound, and in an act of devilishness, I moved my hands from the backs of her thighs to the bottom part of her ass.

The moment my thumbs came into contact with the lips of her sex, I could feel the wetness there, saturating her.

"You want to sit on my cock?" I asked her, widening her thighs with my hands until I could slip my two thumbs between the folds of her sex. "Or do you want me to fuck you with my thumbs," I pushed both of them inside of her at once, causing her to squeal. "Until you come?"

She was panting, her hips bucking as she tried to find her release.

I wouldn't let it come, though. Not yet.

She had to answer me first. I returned to playing with her clit.

I grinned when she didn't answer. Though, I knew that it was likely that she couldn't. Not with the way I was filling her pussy as well as sucking on her clit.

"Sway?" I asked, pinching her clit between my teeth lightly before letting it go completely. "What do you want?"

"Your cock," she breathed. "I want your cock!"

The smile that graced my lips was nothing short of triumphant.

"Then take it. Climb on and fuck me, Sway," I ground out, yanking my towel away.

The moment the word 'fuck' left my mouth, she placed a knee on either side of my legs and began lowering herself onto me.

I worked quickly to line my dick up to her entrance, and the moment she felt it where she needed it, she took me inside.

Not fast, at least not at first.

Slow. So slow, that I thought she was literally trying to kill me.

What was it about this woman that had me acting like a horny teenager again?

I hadn't wanted to come like this since I was fifteen and had lost my virginity.

I've had control over my cock and orgasms for years. But the moment she had me fully seated inside of her, I was ready to come. That wasn't me.

I wasn't acting like me.

So…ask me if I cared.

Because there was only one answer to that.

I didn't.

Not one single bit.

"Fuck me, Sway," I urged her, lifting her hips. "Fuck me hard and fast."

She looked a little hesitant, maybe a little nervous, but when my hands went to her breasts, something seemed to click inside of her.

I held on to her breasts as she worked to take us both there.

The round globes of perfectly succulent flesh bounced in my hands as she hurriedly fucked me.

My head fell forward, and I brought Sway's tight nipple to my mouth, pulling the turgid tip between my lips, biting, licking and flicking as I did.

Which only served to push her even faster.

I closed my eyes at some point as I started to hope that I could hold out long enough for her to come, and when I felt her lean forward, pressing both of her breasts into my face as she hugged my neck tightly, I realized that she was just as close—if not closer—than I was myself.

The moment she had purchase on my neck, she started to slam herself down, using her arms around my neck to steady herself.

"Oh, God," her voice quivered in my ear. "Fuck yes!"

I started to come.

My cock swelled, and my release left me in a rush, filling her insides in warm, wet pulses.

Her orgasm overtook her at about the same time, and I cursed loudly as she started to massage me with that sweet pussy.

"Fuck!"

Her pussy rippled, and at one point I feared that she'd make me come again, but just as I was thinking it'd never end, it slowly waned until nothing else remained but some very delicious aftershocks.

The silence that followed was blissful.

So blissful, in fact, that I wasn't sure I ever wanted to leave this place.

"Son of a whore, but that was bloody brilliant."

We both froze and looked over our shoulders, but there was nothing there that we could make out through the darkness.

"Who is that?" she whispered.

Then she slapped me on the chest.

"Stop laughing," she ordered.

I couldn't help it.

I really couldn't.

There was literally nothing that could be done at this point *but* to laugh.

"I can't believe you made us do this outside. How much do you think he could hear?" she whispered.

"All of it!" came the British accent once again.

I winced.

"This is about as private as the room we were just in," I whispered to her. "There's nothing you can do on this porch that anyone can see. Look at the walls. They're enclosed and separated by about a foot and a half of concrete."

She shook her head.

"Let's go inside. Maybe order some dinner." She stood, leaving me feeling bereft.

Then a thought occurred to me.

"Shit!" I exploded. "We have to go!"

Sway's confusion was evident on her face, and I was quick to explain.

"I promised one of the rookies on the other team that I'd have dinner with him. We're supposed to be there in like twenty minutes."

Sway followed me, and without a word, she got dressed and had dinner with us.

And as I watched her that night and during the next day, I realized that I was falling in love with this woman.

Hard and fast.

It was a feeling that hit me like that fastball straight to my throat. I couldn't breathe, and I wasn't sure I would ever be the same again.

CHAPTER 15

This year I will drink more wine and wear less pants.
-Sway's New Year's resolution

Hancock

I jogged up to the stadium's side entrance that the players used and yanked the door open, practically falling inside the moment I felt the cool air.

"Motherfucker it's hotter than a cow's balls outside," I gasped, leaning against the first wall I came to.

"That was eloquent," Gentry drawled, arriving just after me.

"Fuck you," I grumbled. "Why the fuck do I run with you, anyway?"

"Because you don't want to be fat like your brothers," Gentry shot back, reminding me exactly why I ran with him. "Well, all brothers but one."

I didn't want to be fat like my brothers.

Or my dad.

Not that they were fat, per se. But they did have beer bellies, and I knew for a fact that I would have one if I stopped working out and forcing myself to eat healthily.

I had a weak spot for beer and fried chicken.

I was a Southern boy, born and raised.

I liked my food fried, my beer cold, and my ladies soft.

Like Sway.

Gentry threw his arm out and caught me side armed in the shoulder.

"Let's go," he ordered. "Now, we have to go see your cute, little…"

We both stopped when we heard the anguished scream, then started running.

Rhys, the third baseman, came running out of the room like his ass was on fire.

"What the fuck, man?" I asked, stopping him before he could get too far.

"Something happened to George's kid. I think…I think he died," Rhys explained quickly, his face a mask of worry. "He's pulling his goddamned hair out. I think we need to call 911, but I don't have a phone."

I slammed Rhys on the arm with the side of my fist.

He was a good man, but he didn't know how to handle emotions. He was like a fucking blank wall. Getting the man to crack a goddamn smile was like pulling teeth. I wasn't sure he even comprehended half the jokes that were said. Mostly because he had to be a fucking robot not to laugh at one of them.

And for him to think that George needed an ambulance was telling.

George, or Furious George, was the six-foot-six powerhouse who was the biggest man on the team.

He played centerfield and was damn excellent at what he did.

Pitch Please

His hitting average was almost unheard of, and he was an all-around great baseball player.

Furious George, though, had a problem.

His temper, even on the best of days, wasn't so great.

In fact, he'd lose it over just about anything if it rubbed him wrong.

"Gentry," I pointed to Rhys. "Go get the truck."

Gentry nodded and darted off, sprinting as if he hadn't just run four miles with me.

I headed into the locker room, freezing at seeing a man as big and full of life as George was, on his knees crying.

For real, tears were streaming down the big man's cheeks like they were never going to end.

"George," I said roughly. "George. Tell me what's wrong."

He didn't answer at first. In fact, I had to repeat myself three more times before I finally got anything out of him.

And what I heard was enough to gut me forever.

"My boy," he cried. "He was in an accident, and they don't expect him to live."

"Which hospital?" I barked, trying to break through to him.

George's back stiffened, and he turned his face up to mine.

And that's when I saw the pure devastation there.

The anguish was apparent, but he seemed to shelve some of it, compartmentalize it until he had his head on straight enough to function.

"They flew him to Dallas. *Children's*," he answered, his voice breaking halfway through.

"Let's go," I ordered, snapping my fingers at him.

The ride to Children's wasn't very comfortable.

The entire time George kept his eyes straight ahead, staring blankly at the road in front of us.

I'd had to pee for at least the last hour of our drive from having downed two bottles of water right before the incident, but I wasn't stopping.

Not until we got to the hospital.

"He was hit by a drunk driver," George muttered into the quiet cab.

My heart fell.

I didn't dare reply.

I didn't want him going ape shit in the truck with me. I also didn't want him to talk if he didn't want to.

What I wouldn't do for Gentry to be here right now.

I'd intended for him to come. Gentry was the smooth talker. The man that could get anyone to talk.

But George had taken one look at him and told him to go away.

Gentry had looked at me for guidance, and I'd shook my head, telling him without words not to bother.

Which led us to now.

Two hours into our silent trip.

"He was riding his bike with my ex-wife at the park, and the fucker lost control of his vehicle at the stop sign. Instead of turning right where there was a ditch, he turned left, right into my kid who only learned how to pedal the wheels of his bike last week."

Tears burned my eyes.

The devastation in George's voice was killing me.

I wanted to offer him words, but he knew, just as well as I did, that they would be empty.

I didn't know if his kid would be alright. I didn't know if George was ever going to see him again.

So again, I kept silent.

If anything, I could give him the knowledge that I was present. I was there for him if and when he needed me.

My phone started to vibrate against my leg, interrupting my thoughts as I drove.

My phone had rung no less than fifteen times since I'd gotten into the car with George.

I let it go to voicemail.

Again.

Three of the calls I knew were Sway. Two of them I knew were my mom.

Sway and I had played with my phone a couple of nights ago and made everyone I knew that called me specific vibrations that would alert me as to who was calling without looking at the display.

"This is the exit," George pointed, no inflection at all in his voice.

I signaled and took the exit, then started to wind my way through the crazy amount of downtown Dallas traffic.

I didn't drop him off at the front like most would.

I parked, knowing he'd scare the staff if he went in there with the way he was acting.

The moment I parked and got out, I got in front of George and turned, halting him in his progression to the door.

"Stop."

George was three inches taller than me, and although it didn't seem like much on paper, when you were looking up into the eyes of a six-foot-six man who was bound and determined to bowl you over, it was quite intimidating.

"Look at me." I ordered.

George looked at me, his hands clenched into fists.

"Take a deep breath."

He took a deep breath.

"Right now, your son and your ex-wife don't need to see the crazy," I ordered. "Your boy needs his dad, and your ex-wife needs her baby's father. Don't go in there flipping out on the first person you see, okay?"

I knew George. I'd spent the last six years of my life playing with him.

He didn't get the name 'Furious George' for no reason.

I also knew, for a fact, that he was still very much in love with his ex-wife, and although I didn't know the circumstances of their parting, I knew they both still spent quite a bit of time together. She came to his games. He went to her softball games, although they weren't professional ball games.

They literally spent time together like husband and wife, minus the actual husband and wife designation.

"Thank you," he said, and without another word, he walked around me and started into the hospital.

I made it to the receptionist first, making sure that George wouldn't get a chance to bark at anyone if I could help it.

"Micah Hoffman," I said to the man. "He was brought in by air-med about two hours ago by my count."

The man's face widened as he looked at me and George.

I knew what was coming, and I shook my head minutely at the man.

This wasn't the time to be recognized, and luckily the man caught on and turned back to the computer.

"He's in surgery. That's on floor two. Use the bank of elevators right there, press number two, and when the doors open, turn to the right and the waiting room will be directly on your left," he instructed.

I nodded.

"Thank you."

We followed the man's directions, and the moment we showed in the waiting room, George's wife—ex-wife—barreled toward him.

"Georgie!" she wailed, throwing herself at him.

George's arms surrounded her, pulling her in so closely that there was no space at all between them.

They both buried their faces into each other's necks and started to cry.

I backed away to give the two of them privacy, stopping at the end of the hall where there were no rooms or doors.

Once I was far enough away, I pulled out my phone, ignored the missed calls, and immediately called Gentry.

"I got him here," I said the moment he picked up.

"Good," Gentry exhaled. "Any news?"

"No." I shook my head. "When we got here the guy at the front desk said he was in surgery."

Gentry exhaled. "It's awful."

It was.

"I've had calls from Sway and your mom. You might want to call them back," Gentry continued. "They didn't tell me why they called, but they both know that you had to take George to Dallas."

I nodded. "Thanks. I'll call them back now."

The moment we hung up, I scrolled to Sway's name and tapped it.

It rang twice before she answered.

"Is he okay?" she begged the moment she answered.

"I don't know," I admitted. "He's still in surgery."

She let out a shaky breath.

"Fuck," she cleared her throat. "Your mom called me."

"Yeah?" I asked in confusion. "Why?"

I could feel her hesitation, and my stomach started to sour.

"Something happened."

"What happened?" I pushed.

"Something overseas. Your dad got a call. They think your brother was hurt on a mission." she said quietly.

My stomach dropped for a second time that day and stayed somewhere around my knees.

"I'll call you back."

The moment I hung up, I called my mother.

"What's going on?" I asked the moment she picked up.

My mother started crying.

"Mom!" I barked, not liking the hesitation.

"Your brother...he was hurt over there...they said," she moaned between crying jags.

"Give me the phone, woman," my dad's barking command broke in.

I took a deep breath and waited.

My dad wasn't the most eloquent man in the world, but I knew he'd get all the information across without having to hear my mother crying her eyes out.

"Your brother and his team were on a mission when they were ambushed. Three of his teammates are dead. Two were captured, and one was injured. That's the one they think is your brother."

"They think?" I pushed.

"Corvallis couldn't give us much more than that," Dad explained.

Corvallis was a family friend, and the leader of the team of misfits. When Corvallis left the Air Force, he lured my brother away, too. Helping him join the world of black ops, and together, they formed a covert organization that even I didn't know that much about.

My dad and Corvallis had served together, and that bond was still as tight now as it was thirty years ago, though somewhat strained when Corvallis didn't give us all the information we wanted, when we wanted it.

Corvallis had promised to keep an eye out on Hannibal, and he'd done so, giving us updates even though we didn't sometimes like those updates. Like now.

"Where's he at?" I croaked.

"Germany, for now," Dad said. "Gonna head out later tonight."

I rubbed my sternum, suddenly feeling so much turmoil rolling around in my chest that I didn't know what to do.

"The All-Star break is coming up next week. I'm going to play tonight's game, and tomorrow's," I cleared my throat. "Then I'll have a few days to come."

"That's perfectly reasonable, Son," Dad agreed. "I believe they might even transfer him again before then, so it'd be good to wait a few days to come out so we know where he's headed next."

I looked blankly at the long hallway, not seeing anything in particular.

"Love you, Pop."

"Love you too, Son. Be good."

The familiar saying made a small smile kick up the corner of my mouth, but just as quickly, it fell.

Dad used to say that to Hannibal and I, but he really was talking more to Hannibal than me. Hannibal and I were okay apart, but together we were atrocious. Though, most of that was because Hannibal was crazy.

Not crazy, crazy, but crazy as in he would do anything crazy.

"You better be okay, fucker," I whispered a quiet prayer. "You better be okay."

***

I walked into the dugout two minutes before game time.

I'd missed the national anthem. I'd missed the opening pitch that I normally caught. I also almost missed my kiss from Sway.

Though that was something I collected on despite the fact that the whole entire world was probably watching us.

At this point in the day, I was tired of everything. I was literally on the verge of a mental breakdown, and I needed my woman.

"You okay?" she asked once the kiss ended.

She ran her hand over my hair, then smoothed her soft fingers over my beard.

"No," I told her truthfully. "I'm about as far from okay as a man can get right now."

She closed her eyes, and then opened them. "He'll be okay."

He would.

That I knew.

The question was whether he would be the same.

"Ready to play ball, boys?" Coach Siggy bawled.

He looked at me specifically, and I nodded.

"Ready."

We weren't ready.

We sucked it up.

Bad.

Gentry hit three players. I missed the goddamned ball more often than I caught it. Rhys was fucking up and making errors right along with us, and we didn't get a single hit the entire game.

"Good game," the other team's first baseman said as he collected the bat that was laying on the ground next to my feet.

I looked over at him, sweat dripping down my face and into my eyes.

"Yeah," I lied.

He slapped me on the back. "How's the kid?"

"Out of surgery. He's alive…but they're not sure if he'll make it yet or not."

"Fuckin' A," he murmured quietly. "Keep us updated, okay?"

I nodded once and watched him leave, wondering if the entire world was aware of what had happened to George only hours before the game.

But they were only aware of one part of the turmoil I was feeling right then, and hopefully, they would never be the wiser.

***

Four days later

I knew the minute I picked up the phone that something was wrong.

Terribly wrong.

"Hello?" I answered, disrupting not just my sleep, but Sway's and my dog's as well.

"I know it's late," my dad's voice broke into the quiet. "But we need to talk."

"What?" I asked, sitting up. "Is Hans okay?"

My dad cleared his throat.

"There's not an easy way to say this…but your brother isn't the man we came to see. The man that we've been giving you updates on over the last week was a young man named Easton Monroe. He's a part of your brother's team…but he's not your brother."

"Then if he's not there, and not one of the dead…where the hell is he?"

"That's the problem." My dad's voice was tired. "We don't know."

CHAPTER 16

Mommy, when I grow up I want to be a total bitch like you.
-Hancock, Age 7

Hancock

"Listen," I told our general manager. "I'm not playing in the game. I don't want to. I'm not paid to play in the game. And it's not in my contract that I am required to play the All-Star Game. So, you can kiss my ass. Find someone else to use."

"This isn't something where we can just find another player to use. This is something that you were voted into. It's good exposure for our young team. This is fucking perfect," Ernie continued as if I'd never spoken.

"Ernie," I looked at him. "I'm not doing it. Got it?"

"Hancock…"

"Not. Doing. It."

Ernie's lips pursed. "Just think about it, okay?"

He left before I could refute his comment, and I turned to glare at the man's back.

"I'm not doing it!" I bellowed.

"Can you turn down a position in an All-Star Game?" Sway's quiet voice from behind me had me starting.

I turned to see her standing behind me, arms crossed and eyes studying me like I was an interesting bug.

She'd heard, and I wanted to groan.

Instead, I turned and studied her before speaking, my words tight and clipped.

"I just did," I pointed out the obvious, my words angrier than I'd intended them to come out. "Did you not notice?"

Her lips pursed.

"Getting mad and throwing attitude at me isn't the way to go about doing this. I know you're hurt. I know you're scared. And I know you're not meaning to, but you need to seriously stop acting like an ass to everyone. It's not good for your team, and frankly, I don't like it. You're not you." Sway's arms crossed over her chest.

My eyes narrowed.

"You don't like it?" I snapped.

She shook her head.

"You've got nothing to do with this. You don't know my brother. You don't even know me all that well," I growled, the words falling from my lips before I could stop them. "So maybe I should just take my bad attitude and stay the fuck away from the people who don't like listening to me."

Her mouth dropped open, and her face paled.

But I'd already gone too far, and I wasn't in the mood to apologize, even though it was obvious that I was acting like an ass, and she was only trying to help.

Regardless, I couldn't do anything. I couldn't apologize.

My head wasn't on straight.

My mind was in the fucking clouds as I thought about where my brother could be. Whether he was okay. Wondering if I would ever see him again.

It was literally all I could think about over the last couple of days, and I didn't see it getting any better. Not until I had some fucking answers.

Answers that I intended to get tonight when I spoke with Corvallis.

Corvallis, who'd reluctantly taken the meeting with me.

Lucky for me, and unlucky for him, he had business in the city to attend to.

He'd, of course, tried to get out of it, claiming a busy schedule.

I'd pulled the godson card, though, and he'd had no choice but to meet with me.

I was sure he was going to try to beat around the bush when it came to Hannibal's whereabouts—because there was not a single doubt in my mind that he knew exactly where he was—but I wasn't going to let him.

I was going to leave that place with the knowledge of where my brother was, and I wasn't going to let him play me.

He knew something, and I was damn sure going to find out.

"That was kind of harsh," Gentry drawled. "She was telling the truth, you know."

I turned my head to glare at Gentry.

"Fuck you."

His brows rose.

"You just told the girl you were falling in love with to leave you the fuck alone," Gentry pointed out.

I glared at him.

"I most certainly did not say that," I countered.

Not in so many words, anyway.

"And I'm not in love with her."

Gentry's brows rose even higher.

"You're so full of shit I can see it coming out of your ears." He crossed his arms and leaned against the locker that was directly beside mine. "And your fucking face is telling me something completely different than your words."

I sighed.

"I'm not in the mood, Gentry."

"You better get in the mood, or you're going to lose one of the best things you've ever had in your life—and that's saying something since you're currently making forty-two million dollars over a five-year period," Gentry argued.

I shrugged my shoulders and brought my hand to my face.

"I can't fucking think straight."

Gentry continued to stay silent, and I pinched the bridge of my nose.

"I fucking love her, okay?" I growled. "Stop it."

Gentry chuckled.

"Your brother's gonna love her."

If my brother came back was left unsaid, but we were both thinking it.

"When's your meeting with Corvallis?"

"How did you know about my meeting with Corvallis?" I questioned, picking up my glove—which had miraculously turned back up after the last game.

"I overheard you speaking with him outside of Sway's office," Gentry answered, picking up his own glove.

We were headed out to toss the ball around—something that I hadn't intended to do. Not until after the All-Star break, anyway. We only had one week off—well, four days and five nights—and I usually used this time as a breather for the rest of the season. In the years since I'd been playing professionally, I'd never once picked up a baseball or my glove, but this time I needed the release. Needed the freedom it would allow my mind as I did something meaningless like tossing the ball around with my best friend.

Tossing the ball around was a stress reliever for me, and Gentry knew it.

"I haven't had my meeting with Corvallis," I grumbled. "Later this afternoon, actually."

"Didn't I hear you tell Sway and her friend, Ember, that you would go to dinner with them tonight?" Gentry asked as he tucked his glove underneath his arm.

"Yeah," I mumbled.

"Hmmm," Gentry hummed, leading the way out to the field.

We didn't practice on the same field that we played on. The field we played our games on was off limits, even to the players, during off time such as now.

Which was why we headed in the opposite direction we usually took, which led us straight past Sway's office.

The moment I was close enough to her door, I could hear her talking.

"No, I'm going to have to cancel on you tonight. I'm not feeling well."

My mouth thinned as I turned the corner into Sway's office, easily slipping the phone from underneath her hand and placing it against my ear.

"Sway's lying. We can't go because my Godfather is in town, but I want to reschedule." I declared. "I was being an asshole, and she's mad at me."

"Ooookay," Ember drawled. "If you change your mind, we're gonna go to Peter Pan's."

Peter Pan's was a new pub in the heart of downtown Longview, and something that I'd been looking forward to trying.

What I was not looking forward to dealing with, however, was the angry look in Sway's eyes.

"Thanks. Bye," I murmured, tucking the phone into my shorts pocket.

My eyes automatically found Sway's angry ones, and it took everything I had not to laugh at her.

"I'm sorry," I told her bluntly. "I've been acting an ass, and I shouldn't be taking it out on you."

Her face automatically softened.

"It's okay," she lied.

"No, it's not," I grumbled. "But it is what it is. I'm going to try really hard to stop being a jerk, but it's likely that I'm still going to be pretty pissy until I find him."

Sway's eyes showed every single emotion that powered through her mind, and I could concur with a few of them. The feeling of the unknown wasn't the best thing in life to deal with, especially when it came to my brother.

Pitch Please

"Where are you going?" She touched the glove with a single finger, and I licked my lips.

"We're headed out to the practice field to toss the ball around. Do you want to join us?"

Her eyes widened.

"I literally suck at baseball."

A grin tipped up the corner of my mouth.

"Don't worry. You have the best pitcher and the best catcher in the league showing you the ropes."

Twenty minutes later found us staring at Sway in horror.

"You can't step out of the way of the ball," I told her. "Otherwise it'll throw off your entire trajectory."

"But if I don't move out of the way, I might miss the ball, or it might hit me in the face," Sway countered.

"But how do you know if you don't even try?" Gentry asked. "You've done that the entire time we've been out here!"

Sway tossed a glare at him.

"I'll have you know, Gentry, that I've not dropped a ball yet. Can you say the same?"

I choked on the water I was drinking and stopped long enough to let a bellow of laughter out.

"That was because Mr. Handsy over there shoved his hands down your pants right in front of me," Gentry challenged. "How do you expect me to catch a ball when he's busy feeling you up?"

Sway's eye twitched.

"He wasn't doing anything in my pants," Sway said. "He was fixing my belt!"

Gentry's brow rose.

"Yeah…" he rumbled. "And he needed to stick his hands down, not just your pants, but into your underwear, to do it?"

Sway sighed.

"Shut up," Sway grumbled, her face going beet red as she did.

I grinned at their back and forth.

"What time do you have to leave?" Gentry changed the subject, turning to me. "It's already four. When are you meeting Corvallis?"

"Corvallis?" Sway asked in surprise. "Your godfather?"

I shot Gentry a glare.

"He's going to hopefully give me some information about Hannibal," I told her evasively.

Sway stared at me.

"You're meeting him before we go out to dinner." she stated.

I nodded my head.

"Yeah," I looked at the watch on my wrist. "He's supposed to come here, though."

"Hmmm," she murmured. "Do you mind if I sit in on this meeting? I'd like to meet him."

I tossed another glare in Gentry's direction.

"Catch," I told her, tossing the ball high and slow.

She, of course, moved out of the way and then caught it, firing off the ball right back at me like a fuckin' pro.

At least she could throw. She still needed a lot of work on catching.

"Nice," I caught it and tossed it in Gentry's direction.

We were in a triangle, and Gentry and Sway were close, while I was fairly far away.

Once I caught the ball that Gentry threw back at me, with less heat than I was used to from him, I threw it high and slow to Sway.

We did this for about ten more minutes in silence before someone interrupted us.

"This her?"

I turned to find Corvallis, or better known as Leslie, my godfather, staring at Sway with accusation.

Sway wasn't one to back down, though, and she caught the ball Gentry let slip through his fingers.

"Are you Leslie right now, or Corvallis?" I asked him.

There was a difference between the two men.

Corvallis was the ex-military badass that obeyed orders. He had the United States of America's best interest at heart.

Leslie was my godfather. He gave me what I wanted, when I wanted it. He had *my* best interests at heart. *Hannibal's* best interests at heart.

Leslie sighed and turned to me, dismissing Sway.

"You know exactly who I am, boy," Leslie countered. "I just wanted you to introduce your woman to me."

He said 'your woman' like it was something dirty.

Sway froze where she was walking toward us and frowned hard at Leslie.

Gentry caught up to her and placed a hand on her arm briefly, and jealousy surged in my gut at the thought of my best friend touching her. I knew in my heart that he would never do anything inappropriate with her, but my head and my heart weren't always in sync, and sometimes illogical thoughts made their way into my mind.

"How about we go talk for a minute. Sway, why don't you go inside and give me a few minutes with my godfather," I ordered, gesturing to the side entrance to the building that we'd exited from half an hour before.

Sway pursed her lips, but she chose not to argue.

Instead, she followed closely behind Gentry as she walked inside, giving Leslie a wide berth.

The moment the doors closed on them, I turned my glare on him.

"What the fuck, Leslie?" I barked.

Leslie winced.

"I've had a bad day," he tried to excuse his actions.

I waved my hand in the air.

"Sway isn't one of your men. She isn't me, and she isn't Hannibal. She also isn't dad. She's a woman. You have to treat her as such. She's delicate and doesn't know that you're a dickhead at heart," I snapped.

Leslie's mouth twitched.

"She's cute," he observed.

She *was* cute.

Exceptionally so.

I also knew she'd be sexy as hell in a gown at the end-of-the-season awards banquet that I planned to take her to in a few months.

I also couldn't wait to peel that dress off her supple body and devour her afterwards.

"I realize that sometimes you can't help it, but how about you start off on the right foot here. She's it," I informed him bluntly.

"She's it?" he looked startled.

I nodded.

"She is," I confirmed.

"You've known her what…twelve days?" he asked sarcastically.

"A few months, actually," I admitted. "Which you know, because I told you about her the moment I met her that first day."

Leslie's mouth tightened, and then released as he allowed himself to smile.

"I've been going back and forth all day with people that'll have my ass if I talk to you, and I'm not in the best headspace. But I'm willing to check my suspicions and make nice if you'd like to introduce us this time," Leslie uncrossed his arms.

"You'll tell me what's going on?" I hoped.

He sighed.

"Yeah."

Relief washed through me.

"Thank you."

CHAPTER 17

Nothing inspires the words 'fuck off' like someone telling me I need to watch my language.
-things you probably shouldn't say to an umpire

Sway

I pulled out my secret stash of Oreos and dipped them into my Dr. Pepper.

When I was nervous, I ate.

It was a bad habit that I was never able to kick, and I was making it even worse by adding Dr. Pepper to the mix and dunking my cookies in it.

It was a super weird thing that I started doing when I was in high school, and it'd been something I continued to do when I got stressed out to this day.

Usually, I managed to use milk to dunk my cookies in.

Dr. Pepper had been out of necessity one day, and I'd found out that it was almost ten times better than milk, and I had to force myself not to do it since I knew it was a fattening habit that I definitely didn't need.

"Wow, you're actually here?" Sinclair said snottily, bringing my attention away from my cookie dunking to the door where he stood looking at me with a curl of his lips.

"Yes, I'm here," I said, dropping the cookie into the trashcan beside my desk so he wouldn't see what I was doing in my drink. "Can I help you with something?"

It wouldn't do to have someone know my secret shame.

Sinclair's face pinched.

"Absolutely not," he replied jovially. "Just surprised me to see you where you belong for once."

I clenched my teeth.

"In that case, if you don't mind, would you close my door on your way out?"

I gritted my teeth when his eyes lit with humor.

"I met someone yesterday, and we bonded over our mutual dislike of you." He continued as if I hadn't asked him to leave.

"Is that right?" I asked, leaning back in my desk chair, my Dixie cup full of Dr. Pepper in my hand. "And who might that be?"

His eyes lit with an inner light that set me on edge.

"We didn't know that we hated the same person, you see. We were just discussing our reasoning for being in a bar at the same time," he smiled. "It was funny, because we both said your name at the same time. It was like fate."

"And why, might I ask, was my ex drinking at a bar?" I guessed that was who he was speaking of, seeing as I was pretty sure nobody actively hated me but him. "And what have I done to you to warrant you discussing me like that with a practical stranger?"

I honestly didn't care why he was drinking, or why Langston was drinking for that matter.

In fact, it didn't bother me one bit that I pissed people off. What did bother me, though, was that I hadn't done anything to either one of them to be pissed off at me for in the first place.

I was genuinely a nice person.

It wasn't often that I pissed anyone off, let alone these two men.

Add in the fact that I'd instantly drawn the ire of a man who obviously meant a lot to Hancock, and I wasn't in a good place.

"Well, I went to management, again, and mentioned your obvious love affair with a player, and they didn't do a damn thing about it. Again."

"Again?" I tested the word, finding an instant dislike for it. "You've gone to them before over this?"

"It specifically says in the contract that you're not to fraternize with fellow staff or players."

My mouth tightened.

I'd read that part of my contract, of course, but at the time it hadn't occurred to me that I'd fall in love with a player. *Who knew Hancock Peters would even give me the time of day?*

"Piss off the star player of the team," came an amused voice. "And you lose him. He has thirty other teams in the league that would kill to have him, and he has the money to break his contract. Do you really think they'll be stupid enough to listen to your useless quibbling instead of letting their star player have what he so obviously wants?"

Sinclair stiffened and turned, and that's when I saw Hancock staring at Sinclair like he was about to murder him. His godfather, Leslie Corvallis, was standing beside him, staring at Sinclair like he was a bug that he was about to step on with his dirty, steel-toed boot.

I stood up, bringing my handful of cookies and my Dr. Pepper with me.

"Hancock! Mr. Corvallis! Hi!"

Hancock's lips twitched, and he turned his angry gaze to me.

His eyes took in my disheveled, harried expression, the cup in my hand and the cookies clenched in the other, and then clenched his jaw once more.

"I suggest you leave and don't come back for a while," Hancock murmured quietly. "And if I ever find out that you've harassed Sway again, you'll be gone. Understand?"

Sinclair left without another word, leaving me with two obviously pissed off men.

"What is his malfunction?" Hancock growled.

"The real question is why the hell is Langston complaining about me at a bar?" I questioned. "I haven't done anything to him. In fact, *he* was the one to break up with *me*. I haven't seen him since the day you were sick with strep and at my house."

Hancock sighed.

"I can hire someone to find out why he's acting the way he is," Hancock shrugged.

"Or…" I held up my finger. "I can just ask my mother."

"Your mother?"

I nodded.

"My mother."

"Why would your mother know anything about Langston and why he's drinking at a bar?" Hancock wondered, his eyes going to Leslie who looked just as confused as me.

"Because they go to church together." I rolled my eyes. "And I'll ask her tomorrow. Tonight is for catching up," I smiled. "So, where are we going to eat?"

Pitch Please

***

I made my way into Hancock's bedroom, leaving the men to their discussion that I knew they were wanting to have without me there.

Neither man had been rude about it, nor had they flat out asked me to leave, but every time the discussion strayed toward Hannibal, both men would easily turn the conversation to something else entirely.

It didn't take me long to realize what they were doing.

Though, I was sure they weren't intentionally being rude about it.

I froze when I walked into Hancock's bedroom and found Ruby, Hancock's dog, sitting on the dresser looking out the window.

The six-foot-tall chest of drawers that had nothing else around it that would enable her to get up there very easily.

"Ruby," I called to his dog. "What are you doing up there?"

Rudy turned only her head and looked at me like I was interrupting something important.

Maybe I was. Maybe she had a routine, and I'd interrupted it by deigning to speak to her.

Deciding to leave her alone, I walked into the bathroom, did my business, washed my face and brushed my teeth, before heading back to the bedroom.

This time it was to find Ruby on the bed, staring at me the moment I came out the door.

"I'm glad you got down," I told the dog. "That's pretty dangerous for you to be up there like that. You could get hurt."

Why was I talking to this dog like it was a human, you ask? Because she was exceptionally smart, and by smart, I mean *smart*.

I think she understands every single word I say.

And her eyes…those eyes of hers are beyond intelligent-looking.

It's like the dog had a world of knowledge behind those beautiful pale baby blues.

"You sleeping with me, big girl?" I asked.

In answer, Ruby jumped off the bed, headed over to the door—which she opened with her paw—and immediately walked out.

Shaking my head and wondering if Hancock had gotten the lever door handles for that very purpose, I walked to the door and closed it, ignoring the way the voices carried from the hallway.

The moment I laid down in bed, my eyes closed, and I melted into the soft sheets.

I'd intended to read so I could talk to Hancock when he finished with his godfather, but the moment my eyes closed, I was dead to the world.

That was until two hours later when my eyes opened in the darkness, and I moaned aloud as pleasure started to course through my veins.

CHAPTER 18

I'd do anything with you, anywhere. Except fellatio in a police station. That's probably frowned upon.
-Text from Sway to Hancock

Hancock

"I'll talk to you in the morning," I mumbled, running my hand through my hair as I made my way down the hallway.

I stepped over Ruby's prone body, who didn't even bother pretending like she wanted to move.

That was my dog, though.

Such an asshole.

Leslie's words swirled in my brain.

Mole. Set up. Captured. Torture.

Those four words stood out. Those four words put a lot of extra stress on my plate, and I didn't know what to do with the offer Leslie had made me before I'd left him.

You want to help? I have a way for you to help.

The door to my bedroom was slightly cracked, and I breathed a sigh of relief that it wasn't closed.

I didn't want to wake Sway up. I knew she wanted to know what we'd discussed, but right now I needed to think about what we'd discussed before I said it all aloud. As long as I didn't voice it, maybe it wasn't as serious as Leslie made it sound.

Which was stupid.

It was serious. *Very* serious.

Leslie wouldn't have told me if he didn't think that Hannibal was already gone.

Taken. Held hostage somewhere in a small town in Iraq. Another team is there getting him. I just don't know what kind of shape we're going to find him in once we're finished collecting evidence to do this the correct way. The kidnappers' specialty has been all over the news lately. If we're lucky, they won't decapitate him on national television like they have the last three captives.

I closed the door a little hard, and my eyes went to the bed where Sway stirred.

She was wearing one of my t-shirts. A bright blue Nike one that I'd gotten when I was playing college ball. It was very comfortable. One of those t-shirts that you slipped on after a long, hot day in the sun.

One that you knew wouldn't chafe your sun-burned skin.

Smiling now, instead of feeling the need to cry like a little boy, I moved on silent feet toward the bathroom.

I'd just flipped the switch nearest the shower on, giving me just enough light to do my business, when I heard it.

She mumbled something in her sleep, and I moved toward her.

"Love you," she whispered again, so softly that I wasn't sure if I'd heard her correctly.

"What, baby?" I asked quietly into the darkness.

If she wasn't awake, I didn't want to wake her.

But those words I'd thought I heard were life savers.

They sent a jolt of pleasure through my body, and I wanted to hear her say them again.

"Love you, Hancock," she repeated, just as softly as before.

She wasn't awake.

She sounded drugged out. Her speech was slurred, and her breathing was even and deep.

"I love you, too," I whispered back.

She smiled making my heart warm.

Then she rolled over on the bed, closer to my side now than hers, and shifted.

Her leg went up and out, taking the blanket with her.

Her arms flailed, one going high above her head causing the t-shirt she was wearing to hike up, and the other went to her chest, her hand resting just underneath her breasts.

Her braless breasts.

I licked my lips, my mind focused solely on Sway now, and started walking toward her.

When I was close enough, I leaned over, planting my fists in the bed on either side of her chest.

She didn't stir, her eyes closed tightly, and her breathing still deep and steady.

I studied her face with what little light the one I'd left on in the bathroom afforded me.

Her lashes lay across her upper cheeks, and her mouth was set in the cutest pout I had ever seen on someone who wasn't a child.

Her beautiful hair was fanned around her head, spread out like she'd tossed and turned a lot in the last hour.

And she was hot.

She had a light sheen of sweat on her forehead, which explained why she didn't have any covers over her body like she usually did when she slept.

Normally, she was so wrapped up in the comforter that I didn't have a hope or a prayer to get it away from her.

Over the last couple of days that I'd been staying with her, sleeping with her and holding her at night, I'd resorted to a single sheet that was usually over my legs along with the comforter.

But I couldn't find it in me to complain.

In fact, I quite liked it.

My eyes traveled down her body, zeroing in on her naked lower half.

Why aren't you wearing panties, pretty girl? I wondered silently.

Of its own volition, my hand moved to her exposed thigh and then slowly up.

Her thighs were so smooth and milky that my roughened, tanned hand looked out of place next to it, reminding me that I should go to sleep and leave her alone. We'd all had a really long day. One I wanted to forget if it was possible to do so.

But then she moaned in her sleep, her thighs moving once again, and I couldn't stop myself.

The moment her legs spread wider, almost beckoning me to her in her sleep, I made the move.

My hand went from being a little naughty to extremely naughty in about half a second.

The moment my fingers touched her juicy core, I growled low in my throat.

Watching her face for any signs of waking, I rubbed the pad of my thumb over her drenched pussy lips, being sure to catch her clit with each broad stroke.

My cock was now straining in my sweat pants, and I said a silent prayer of thanks that I'd decided to change into something more comfortable the moment we'd walked in the door.

Because now that I was here, touching Sway's pussy, I found that I quite liked the naughtiness of what I was doing.

If she'd been awake, she'd be participating.

Not that that would be a bad thing, but right then, I liked that I could do what I wanted to her without her reactions battering at my control.

"Mmm," she moaned in her sleep, legs opening even wider.

A grin kicked at the corner of my lips as I crawled up between her thighs, my mouth only inches from the sweetest pussy in the world.

"Sway?" I voiced, the words whispering against the lips of her sex.

She didn't answer, and I moved forward, my cock pressing into the bed, and gave her one single lick from clit to anus.

She shivered but still didn't wake.

"You taste so good," I told her, even though she wasn't awake to hear the words.

I thought that she needed to hear them. Every single time, in case she forgets how much her body makes mine react.

When she still didn't move or react, I wedged my shoulder against her leg to keep it open fully, and brought my fingers up to the entrance of her sex.

"So ready for me," I murmured, my fingers encountering her wetness that was soaking me in her excitement.

My fingers slid in easily, and I didn't stop until I had two digits buried deeply, all the way up to the webbing.

That got a reaction out of her and she gasped.

I knew it wouldn't be long before she woke.

There was no way in the world she could sleep through this.

Or at least I thought, anyway.

But as thirty seconds turned into two minutes, I realized that she must be a very sound sleeper.

I'd witnessed the phenomenon, but having my fingers buried deep in her pussy with my mouth on her clit wasn't like me rolling over in bed and accidentally bumping into her.

"Fuck me," I groaned when her cunt started to ripple in release.

She cried out and rolled, dislodging not only my mouth from her clit, but my fingers from her pussy.

I smiled and stood up, knowing she was awake now, but she did nothing but roll to her stomach and bury her face into my pillow.

Her hips didn't even move. The entire time, she'd laid still, letting me do anything I wanted to do to her.

"Holy shit," I groaned, lifting my fingers to my mouth and licking each one clean while I stepped out of my sweats and crawled up on the bed behind her.

The way she was laying, with one long, luscious leg extended and the other cocked up toward her chest, caused her ass to lift slightly into the air.

Which was perfect, because all I had to do was crawl in between her legs, line my cock up to her sopping pussy and slowly inch my way inside.

She felt like an inferno as I worked my dick inside her, not stopping until my balls were pressed against her clit, and my pubic hair was tickling her ass.

I moved my hand up underneath the shirt, which had ridden up to her chest, and circled one blunt finger around her nipple.

She hissed and tried to move, but the only thing she was able to do was push back on my cock, which shoved me impossibly deeper inside of her, pulling the breath from my chest.

My free hand went to her hip to steady both of us, while my other fingers continued to play with her nipple.

It wasn't long before it was a diamond hard peak, and I longed to pull the tight bud into my mouth while I fucked her hard and fast.

But in order not to wake her up, I moved my hips slowly, gliding in and out of her, oh so gently.

It felt divine.

I'd never felt anything like it in all my years of sexual experience.

But then again, nothing I'd experienced with Sway—sexual or nonsexual—was like any of my other relationships.

She felt hotter around my cock—which was likely due to the fact that I'd never taken another woman bare before. Her pussy was tighter. Her reactions to my mouth, fingers and cock were more intense.

Sway was perfect. Everything I did to her she liked, and everything she did to me I adored.

All of my feelings for her were frightening.

If she ever left me, she'd fucking break me, and I had a feeling that she knew it.

She moved again underneath me, and I froze in my ministrations to see what she wanted to do.

And what she did had me seeing stars.

She moved until her ass was high in the air, and my cock hit bottom inside of her.

The moment the tip of my cock hit the entrance to her womb, she woke.

I could tell in the way she tensed, and then started to force her ass back into the saddle of my hips, that she was enjoying what I was doing to her, too.

"Please," she breathed, her voice husky and raw, heavy with sleep.

Smiling wickedly, I gave her exactly what *I* wanted.

Moving both hands to her hips, I started to pull her back onto me while I snapped my hips forward.

Her ass jiggled each time I thrust, and her head was thrashing within a couple of seconds.

"I like when you're sleeping," I told her gruffly. "You're so soft and willing, letting me do whatever the fuck I want to do to this pretty, delectable body of yours."

Her pussy clamped down on my cock, and I moved faster.

Our skin was slapping loudly in the quiet room, and my balls swung up to tap her clit each time I thrust forward.

"God, yes," she mewled. "Fuck me harder."

I fucked her harder. So hard that I winced at the sting as our flesh met.

That didn't stop me, though. Didn't even slow me down.

Her hands went up to the headboard to hold her steady so I didn't fuck her into the wall, and I continued to thrust like I would die if I didn't get us both where we needed to be.

A place she hit first, with me following closely at her heels.

I didn't know why today was different.

Didn't know why it felt so good. Didn't know why I'd even taken her in the first place while she was sleeping.

But I loved it. Loved every single second of it.

The moment her pussy started to clamp down on my cock, I let go. Poured everything I had in me to give inside of her tight welcoming hole.

Her body collapsed and I followed her down, my hips still jerking involuntarily as I went.

"This was the best wake-up call I've ever received," she panted, turning her face so she could breathe without being smothered by the pillows surrounding her head.

I chuckled. "Happy to be of service any time I feel like it."

She snorted and turned just a little more, placing a chaste kiss against my bearded cheek.

Then her nose curled slightly.

"Your beard smells like my vagina," she mentioned casually.

"I don't know what you're talking about," I murmured, letting my lips trail over her cheek.

"We need to go shower."

"I don't want to go shower. I want to lay here, inside of you, for the rest of my life."

"That'll get kind of awkward when your parents want to see you," she mentioned.

A smile curved the sides of my lips up.

"Yeah, I could see how that could be awkward," I agreed. "But for now, just tonight, I want to lay like this."

I curled her in tighter to me, and then buried my face into the side of her neck.

"There's a line." She pulled away from me. "That I'm not willing to cross."

"What line is that," I moaned when my cock slipped free of her, allowing it to fall heavily against one thigh with a wet slap.

"A line where you sleep with dried vaginal juices on your face all night," she laughed, picking up a pillow that fell to the floor at some point during our lovemaking.

"What if I wanted to save it for later?" I followed her up, heading behind her into the bathroom.

"You don't need to save anything for later," she tossed over her shoulder. "All you need to do is ask, and I'll gladly give you more."

My eyes lit with excitement.

"Yeah?" I teased.

She bent over to turn the water on in the shower, and I licked my lips as I got another glimpse of her pussy, only this time that pussy had my come running out of it.

"Yeah," she confirmed. "Ready and willing whenever you are."

I followed her into the shower, and winced as the hot water hit my skin.

"What is it with you and your hot showers?" I asked mildly, stepping back so it hit my legs first and not my face.

"What's the point of a shower if it's not hot?" she asked.

"There's hot…" I winced as I moved forward so more of my legs were under the direct flow, and continued. "And then there's 'melting my goddamn face off' hot."

She snickered.

"Don't be a pansy."

In order not to be seen as a pansy in Sway's eyes, I gritted my teeth and stepped forward until I was crowded around her body, the piping hot spray that was about fifty degrees too hot, sprayed down on my back and shoulders, running down my body, and likely peeling my skin off with it as it went.

"It feels good once you get used to it," she pointed out.

I dropped my eyes to hers, and grinned.

"As long as you're with me, baby, I can handle just about anything."

CHAPTER 19

It's a joke, not a dick. Don't take it so hard.
-Coffee Cup

Hancock

"You can't do this, Hancock!" Sway screamed. "You're not a freakin' Special Forces guru! You're a goddamned professional baseball player. You've never even been in the military! Seriously, you can't do this! You could die!"

I looked at her, hollowness in my heart.

"You don't understand," I rasped. "If I don't, how is he going to get home?"

She shook her head in defeat.

"I don't know, but I know this isn't the way," she repeated. "Please don't do this."

I shouldered the bag on the bed.

"I love you, you know."

Her eyes closed as a lone tear fell from her cheek.

"I know." Her eyes flipped open. A little louder this time, she repeated it. "I know. And I love you, too. More than anything."

I walked up to her and pulled her in close, my hand at the back of her head, fingers threaded through her long, tangled locks.

"I love you. Don't leave my place. Stay here. Take care of my dog. Wait for me."

Her eyes filled with more tears, and they slowly poured over.

"You couldn't get rid of me if you tried."

"This isn't a mission, Sway," My godfather butted in. "This is just him showing his face. Making people question him, and what they thought was happening."

"There's no way he'll pass as his brother," Sway replied stubbornly. "Anybody that knows who Hancock 'Parts' Peters is will realize this. The tattoos. There's just no way he will pass as his brother."

"We know this. They'll put two and two together very easily," Leslie agreed.

"Then what the hell is this accomplishing?" she pushed. "Why does he even need to go over there at all?"

Leslie sighed and took a seat, resigned now that he was going to have to explain it fully to her like he had to do to me last night.

I'd been in her very position before I'd come to bed last night, wondering how exactly I was supposed to help.

"The men that have Hannibal don't watch baseball. They don't know Hannibal has a twin, and they don't care about anything that's related to America. They have one purpose, and one purpose only, and that's to lay destruction everywhere they go," Leslie explained for the second time in twenty-four hours. "My hope is that getting him seen, out and about, flaunting the fact that he's alive to the people who *thought* he was dead, it'll draw out the people that we know are behind this. The men who have him were hired to 'publicly take care of him' but didn't." I winced at the 'publicly take care of him' part just as I had last night. "When they get nervous, my hope is that they'll make the mistake of contacting whomever is behind our lines that initiated the operation in the first place, and provide us with a chance to catch whomever it is. I also hope they follow up with whomever has him now, and lead us to Hannibal's exact location. We can't do another goddamned mission with enemies at our six. We're not going to survive the next time."

"This is fantastical," she shook her head. "And how do you plan on getting Hannibal from wherever he's at? Do you even *know* where he's at?"

I nodded as Leslie did, too.

"If our sources are correct, we know the general area. We just can't run with it until we know for sure," he paused. "We've been contacted a few times by an informant, and we're investigating those leads. Which has led us to where we're going with Hancock."

"And where is this?" she asked carefully.

Leslie looked over to me, and I looked over to him.

"A weapon's manufacturer for the US."

She rubbed her eyes with clenched fists.

"This is a fucking mess, and I know it's not going to play out like you're hoping it will," she murmured softly.

"Nothing in this business ever does," Leslie gritted out. "You gotta go with the flow, and go where the wind takes you."

Sway sighed.

"If you die," she turned to me. "I'll never forgive you. Never."

My lips kicked up.

"How are you explaining this to your team?" she pushed.

"I have a month of emergency leave I'm taking," I answered. "As far as anyone but you and Coach Siggy knows, I have a pulled groin, and you've ordered me out of the lineup for the next month."

She dropped her head back to rest on my shoulder.

"This is going to get me fired," she told him. "Or worse."

"What could be worse?" I teased.

"I could be working under Sinclair."

My chest started to vibrate as I tried in vain to keep my laughter inside.

"If Sinclair tries anything, I'll get him fired before he can even laugh about it," I promised her, wrapping my hands around her waist and pulling her soft body into my chest.

Once she was where I wanted her, I pushed my bearded chin into the crook of her neck and rubbed.

She giggled and twisted, pulling out of my arms.

"Do you and Hannibal even look like each other?" she narrowed her eyes at me.

I grinned.

"We're twins, baby."

Sway stared at me.

"You have a beard," she glared. "Is his beard as big as your beard?"

My lips twitched.

"Beards grow," I told her. "And no, his beard is longer than my beard."

She moved until she was pressed fully against me.

Once she was in my arms again, she lifted her hand until she cupped my face.

"I didn't think I'd ever hear you admit that somebody else's beard was bigger than yours." She tugged lightly on my beard.

I snorted.

"It's not like I'm admitting his dick is bigger than mine," I pointed out.

Her eyes twinkled. "Maybe I like guys with bigger…beards."

I yanked her in close, then dropped my mouth to hers.

"Be good, girl."

Her eyes sobered, and she leaned forward to place her lips gently against mine.

"I will."

"Love you, Half-Pint."

Her eyes warmed.

"I love you, too, Parts."

CHAPTER 20

Just choked on a carrot stick. See, this is why I don't eat healthy. Cupcakes don't try to kill me while eating them.
-E-mail from Sway to Hancock

Hancock

The moment I stepped down from the plane, men that I knew were my brother's friends surrounded me. His team, as well as another team that knew him almost as well.

Some of them I recognized, some of them I didn't.

"Fucking uncanny," one of them said.

I turned to survey that man.

He was on the shorter side— well, at least compared to my six-foot-three height—and sporting a scar on his face that made him look like he had a permanent scowl.

"What is?" I questioned him.

"The resemblance." He gestured at my face. "Look exactly like him."

"We're identical twins," I pointed out.

The man's face kicked up into his version of a grin—which admittedly wasn't much of a grin due to the scar—and offered his hand to me. "Tim Teague."

"Hancock Peters," I offered him the same.

"It's nice to meet you," he said.

I nodded.

"These men at my back, from left to right, are Park, Crassus, Jimmy and Tucker." He pointed at the four men directly behind him. "We're glad you're here."

I breathed out a sigh of relief.

"I hope I can help."

"Your face has already helped," he told me. "Now we just gotta get you out of those civilian clothes."

I looked down at my jeans and t-shirt, and then up at the tan cargo pants and brown shirt that the rest of them were wearing, and nodded.

"Okay."

We began walking, and I started looking around while I raised one arm to wipe the sweat already pouring down my face.

It didn't escape my knowledge that I was being watched.

It was decided that I'd come into this specific airport because it was the same one that my brother had been taken from on his way back home.

The airport was also in an area overrun by infidels who thought it was their job to scare every person who tried to come through their turf.

"Don't worry about them," the one who was introduced as Tucker threw his arm around my shoulder. "It's good that they're seeing you here. Gotta give them a good show, though."

I elbowed Tucker off my shoulders.

"That's what I was told," I muttered. "But you have some body odor that's really rank, and I'd rather not have it that close to my face."

Tucker laughed, loud and deep.

"You remind me of him," he sobered. "That was something your brother would say."

I shrugged.

"I just hope I can help, and we can get him out," I murmured. "And I only have two weeks to accomplish this, according to Leslie."

"Who?" Tucker asked, opening the door to a Jeep that looked like it had seen better days.

I slid inside, sandwiched in by Tucker and Crassus, and said, "Leslie Corvallis."

"Corvallis' name is Leslie?"

That was from Park, who was driving.

"Yes," I confirmed. "Has been for the last fifty-seven years, too."

Crassus snorted.

"He's gone nine and a half years without telling us that little tidbit. He said we didn't need to know." His lips twisted into a maniacal smile. "I can't wait to tell him I know. Maybe I'll just use it as I address him next time."

"And maybe he'll knock that stupid smile off your face," Jimmy muttered as he looked out the window.

I found my first smile since I got off the plane.

"Yeah, that's Leslie for you," I confirmed. "Though Hannibal's known it all this time. Why didn't you just ask him?"

"Hannibal was sworn to secrecy. Said he would run the risk of losing his balls if he told us."

"Hmmm," I muttered. "That sounds like it'd be enough of a reason for him not to tell."

"And what is he going to do to you when he finds out you told us?" Tucker asked, looking over at me.

"Not a damn thing if he wants to keep his season tickets."

The group chuckled all around me, and I turned my head to stare out the window.

It was like I was in a different world.

There was absolutely nothing but sand.

Sand for as far as the eye could see.

"Usually, we would have to worry about IEDs. But we had the road swept before we came and it's clean. We're free to drive right up to our base," Tucker commented when he saw me looking.

"Do you have any clue where Hannibal is yet?" I ignored the way the word 'IED' tore through me, making my hair stand on end.

I hated that my brother was over there doing that. I was proud as hell of him for doing it, but I didn't understand *why* he was doing it. Why did he feel the need to be here? He had enough money, and even if he didn't, he could go back to the farm and be a stubborn ass like my other brothers as they worked off the land.

Land that they had no clue I'd bought out from under them—which was going to go over like a bag of snakes shoved up their asses.

"We're still fairly firm on the weapons manufacturer," Tucker murmured, looking out the window himself this time.

"Why is it such a big deal for him to be there…other than him being a fucking American?" I asked. "Isn't this guy from America?"

"Yes," Tim chimed in from the front seat. "If he's authorized to be there. This isn't the embassy. This is a private residence. The compound has its own security detail that are there twenty-four seven. The owner also isn't in on this in any way."

"Then why do you think my brother is there?" I pushed.

"Because all our sources are saying he is," he cleared his throat. "And until we're proven otherwise, that's where we're going to keep our eyes trained."

I sensed the subject was closed.

I also sensed that if I pushed it, he not only wasn't going to answer, he would also likely get a little ticked off.

And I didn't want to piss the guy off.

Regardless of my thoughts about myself, I knew I wasn't trained, nor skilled, enough to be here on my own. I may be in good shape. I may know a lot of things…but none of those things would keep me alive in this place.

Sure, I'd give it a good run, but this was a foreign country. This place was completely and utterly new to me, and I was at the mercy of these men.

"You know, I was really looking forward to watching you play ball tonight," Park said for the first time. "I wanted to see how you played against the girl's brother."

A smile turned up the corner of my mouth.

"I'd have blown his ass out of the water, and kissed his sister while he watched," I grinned and turned to stare at the man. "How do you know about her?"

"Everyone knows about her," Crassus pointed out. "The whole freakin' world watches y'all. Sees y'all. Loves y'all."

That made my heart happy, despite knowing that the world knew about me. I hated being in the public spotlight.

"ESPN has this new 'Sway and Parts' watch that they air during the newscast before the sports recap for the day," Tucker added in.

I shook my head.

"That's crazy," I mumbled. "How did I not know that?"

Probably because I was too busy fucking my woman to watch a report on Sports Center about us.

"They asked Sway's brother his opinion on y'all dating, and he said that he had no problem with the hook up. That you seemed like a good guy, and that you were her favorite player since you showed up in the majors. He said that it was only a matter of time," Tucker continued.

That was news to me. Not that Sway had a weird sort of obsession with me, but that her brother approved.

"We're here," Park said as he pulled up in front of an old apartment building that looked to be about eight hundred years old.

But it was nicer than all of the other buildings surrounding it, so I guessed that was something.

"Home sweet home," Tucker grunted as he pushed through the door to what I guessed was the apartment the men were using as their headquarters for the mission.

A very small apartment that looked like it hadn't been cleaned in weeks.

See, I wasn't the cleanest of people, but at least I knew how to throw away a fucking empty beer bottle.

These men, though, seemed to be decorating the room with their empties.

"Don't look so disgusted," Tucker grinned. "You'll get used to it, rich boy."

I laughed.

"This has nothing to do with my being rich, as you put it, and everything to do with the fact that there's Cheetos dust all over the couch and the arm rest where you're sitting." I pointed to the offending materials.

"Hmm, would you look at that," Tucker said as he took a seat in the cheese dust. "Game's on."

My eyes flew to the TV.

"How do you get this?" I asked.

He pointed to a large antenna that was on the balcony, and I hummed in understanding.

"State of the art stuff, thanks to your god-daddy," Tim grunted as he walked to the fridge that was only about ten paces behind the couch, cracked the door and came back out with a beer in his fist.

"That's nice of him, I guess," I murmured, taking a seat in a recliner that looked like something most people would be throwing out. "He's like that, though." I looked around. "So, what do we do now?"

Tucker picked up a remote and hit the red button, and another TV came on next to the game. One that was showing about twenty different camera angles on a gated house. "Now we wait."

***

It took one week, three days, and eight hours of constantly watching the TV, parading myself around in town, and expressing my general annoyance at the situation before something finally happened.

I'd missed seven games, six of which my team had lost, and I was beyond irritated.

A, because I was missing the games and I hated that we were losing them. And B, because the catcher who'd taken my place while I was 'injured' was now trying to take Sway as well.

I'd watched her, time after time, go out on the field when the stupid little fucker acted like he was hurt.

I was now contemplating his death.

I also realized that this kid was a little asshole who needed to be put in his place, that's for damn sure.

He was cocky. He was a shitty batter, and he was going to be getting his ass kicked the moment I got back.

I wanted to go home. The rage inside my chest each time I saw Sway get flirted with by that little cock sucker was enough to cause me heart palpitations.

I wanted my brother home.

I wanted to take a hot goddamned shower that lasted longer than thirty seconds.

I wanted a fucking cheeseburger.

And most of all, I wanted Sway.

The good thing was that later that night, everything in our entire fucking plan seemed to work out perfectly…mostly.

CHAPTER 21

I vow to still grab your butt even when you're old and wrinkly.
-Hancock's wedding vows

Sway

"Why would I want to throw the first pitch?" I asked in confusion. "That's a big thing. I'm a nobody."

"Just do it," Uncle Siggy passed me the ball. "This is the last game in the series against your brother's team. They want you to throw the ball because they like seeing stupid shit like that. Plus, wouldn't it be something if we won against your brother's team, and you had the first pitch?"

I sighed, took the ball from my uncle and started walking toward the mound.

Though the entire scene of throwing the first pitch wouldn't be perfect if I didn't trip going up the steps of the dugout. Oh, and halfway across the field.

My eyes went to home plate where the catcher for our team and the umpire were having a discussion. With both of them already wearing their masks, they had their faces pushed together so they could hear what the other was saying over the noise of the crowd.

"What in the hell?" I muttered, waving at my brother who was standing at the top of the steps watching me.

My brother rose his chin in acknowledgement, and I had the ridiculous thought that I should go over there and mess up the paint underneath his eyes with wet, sloppy kisses.

He'd probably kill me after he was finished dying of embarrassment.

But, since the two men were still deep in discussion, I passed the mound and continued straight toward my brother, who was now watching me with apprehension in his eyes.

"What are you doing?" He asked warily.

I grinned and walked into his arms, which he opened for me once he realized what I was after.

"Love you." He told me.

I grinned, stepped back, then grabbed hold of his head, brought his face down to mine, and pressed my face against his so hard that I knew there was no way the paint hadn't spread.

"You're such a shit!" He laughed, pushing me away.

I wiped my face on the black polo shirt, hoping that I got most of the paint off, and gave him a small wave as I jogged back toward the pitcher's mound.

I looked at my uncle, who watched it all, and waved.

He shook his head and gestured toward the catcher who was now waiting on me.

I arrived at the mound and kicked the chalk bag out of the way before taking my place on the top of the small hill.

I eyed the distance from the plate to where I was standing.

Please don't embarrass yourself. Just throw it hard, right to the catcher. He'll catch it.

Speaking of the catcher, the one behind the plate wasn't the backup who'd been playing since Hancock had left three weeks ago.

No, this one was much bigger.

Much.

But he wasn't Hancock.

Hancock had been tall and stocky.

This guy was tall, but he wasn't nearly as bulked up as Hancock had been.

And what the hell was the deal with the long sleeves in the middle of summer? He wasn't wearing those because he thought they looked good, right?

Where had he come from? Surely if they'd gotten another catcher, they would've told me...*right?*

The catcher waved his hand at me to 'hurry on up,' and I sighed.

Taking one step, I launched the ball at the catcher, and it went right to his glove. He didn't even have to move for it at all. No steps to the side. No ball rolling to his glove.

Hell, no. That just wasn't how I rolled.

It went directly to his glove, straight through the air. *A perfect damn strike!*

As the happiness poured through me that I was able to get it to him without it falling ten feet in front of him like I'd seen some of the other ladies who'd thrown the first pitch do this year, I clapped my hands together and started walking forward.

It was customary to take the ball with you, and that'd been what I was going to do.

When I got to him, he handed me the ball, but stayed in his crouched position.

Once I took it from his hands, the catcher stood, and I waved at him, intending to head to the dugout.

I just couldn't find the same enthusiasm for the game now that Hancock wasn't there.

I'd tried, of course, but without him to watch, the game wasn't nearly as fun.

I'd been watching him since he'd been acquired by the Lumberjacks.

Literally the game did nothing for me anymore.

"Hey!"

I stopped and turned, watching as the catcher started to remove his mask.

"What?" I snapped, somewhat harshly.

Then my breath froze in my chest as those familiar locks of hair came into view.

And the beard.

Oh. My. God. I know that beard!

"Hancock!"

Hancock caught me, and then promptly lost his footing as we both fell back to the dirt.

It'd only been two weeks.

But it felt like two years.

Literally, I was stupid. I shouldn't be crying right now.

But I'd been so worried about him, and I hadn't heard from him in so long that my worries and doubts started to take over.

The crowd around us went wild when Hancock's mouth touched mine, and I smiled as I pulled back.

"This is very inappropriate," I murmured happily.

"I had to get my kiss before the game," he teased me. "And you never came back to your office or these extreme measures wouldn't have been necessary."

My face broke out into a grin.

"That's ridiculous. I've been in my office all afternoon!" I informed him haughtily.

He laughed.

"I know."

"How do you know?" I pushed off of him.

He didn't take the hand I offered him. Instead, he stood up, and then wrapped his arms low around my ass, lifting me up off my feet as he swung me around and then carried me off the field.

"I was taking care of a few matters," he grunted, setting me down in the mouth of the dugout.

"And what might those matters be?" I asked as he started to back away.

Players started to file out of the dugout around me even though I was standing in the middle of the stairs, but I kept my eyes focused on Hancock.

"Nothing for you to worry your pretty little head about right now."

Shaking my head in bemusement, I headed down the steps, knocking shoulders with my uncle as I went, and took my normal seat.

I did happen to notice that Croft—the backup catcher—was at the very end of the dugout with his face turned toward the field.

His eyes were on Hancock, watching every move he made.

And I noticed a bruise forming under his right eye.

What the hell had happened to him?

I couldn't find it in me to care at that point, though.

Hancock had made me so extremely happy that I couldn't freakin' contain it.

I was literally bouncing in my seat as I watched the boys get ready to play ball.

So fucking happy.

CHAPTER 22

Maybe serial killers are just regular killers on a low carb diet.
-Chinese Fortune

Sway

The moment Hancock's foot hit home plate, I was on my feet.

"Yes!" I exclaimed. "Go, Hancock! Woo hoo!"

I might, or might not have, been very excited.

So excited, in fact, that I was literally wiggling enthusiastically for Hancock to make his way toward me.

But he was waylaid by his teammates who caught him up around the hips and lifted him straight off his feet.

The moment he was up in the air, someone moved him so he was parallel to the ground, and the entire team was tossing him around like he was a fuckin' child.

Though, I could see their exhilaration.

The team had lost all of their games over the last two weeks that they'd been back from the All-Star break except for one.

And the minute Hancock shows back up, they not only win, but they knocked five home runs out of the park. One was even a grandslam.

Two of which were hits by Hancock himself.

The team, from what I could tell, didn't appear to be mad at him.

All except Croft, that was.

Croft was pissed that as soon as he started playing, the team started losing, which he made a point of complaining to me about each time they lost, and he had to come to me for an ice bath—for sore muscles that I damn well knew weren't all that sore.

I'd passed him off to Sinclair, and I'd seen their heads bobbing back and forth as they spoke softly to each other.

I knew there was something going on between them, just like there was right now. The two of them were huddled together, talking quietly to each other instead of Croft participating in the team celebration that was happening on the field.

Not that I could blame him. I would've been upset too if the star player came back and immediately put me out of the job.

So yes, I could sympathize, but I didn't get the reason for his hostility in the first place.

And having Sinclair in the mix was downright troubling.

"Sway?" Siggy called.

I turned to find him staring at me in confusion.

"What?" I asked.

"Games over. You ready to go?" he asked.

I turned to look, and was surprised to find that no one was on the field anymore except for Hancock, who was talking to reporters.

"Yes," I nodded my head. "What…"

I stopped when I noticed my brother come up behind the reporter who was interviewing Hancock, a blond male in his forties, and make the thrusting hip gesture as he brought his fingers—in the shape of a V—to his lips and flicked his tongue out.

Hancock's head tilted, and he tried for all he was worth to continue with the interview, but it didn't take long before he burst out laughing.

Which Siggy and I did as well.

"That boy can get anyone to laugh," Siggy chuckled. "You going over there?"

I nodded.

"Yeah," I confirmed. "I think Mom and Dad are in the stands over on the visitors' side. I might go talk to them while I wait for the interview that I know is about to happen between my brother and Hancock. Are you going to dinner with us?"

"Negative," Siggy denied. "I'm tired, and your brother gives me a headache."

I snorted.

"Teller gives everyone a headache," I pointed out. "That doesn't stop us from going out to dinner with him, though."

"Yeah, well I've been battling a headache for two weeks now. I'm hoping it'll stop tonight," he grumbled, picking up his bag and heading for the locker room.

I didn't stop him.

I knew he was on edge.

Everyone was.

Hancock leaving—warranted or not—had thrown everyone.

It'd take some time for everything to go back to the way it was.

Shaking my head clear of thoughts about how it felt to have Hancock gone, I took the steps to the field and crossed it, making my way over to my parents, who were still seated and watching my brother and Hancock, who were just to the right of where they were sitting.

Giving them a wide berth so I wouldn't interrupt them on national television, I moved to the padded wall that was separating the stands from the field and clasped my dad's hand.

"Hey, Daddy," I called. "How are you doing?"

Dad's eyes filled with love as he stared at me.

"I'm doing good, baby. But I'm not sure whether I should be happy that my team won or sad that your brother lost," he laughed.

I giggled.

That was true.

I didn't know what to say or do either.

On one hand, I was sad that my brother lost, but on the other, I was excited that my team won.

It was a lose-lose situation.

"Did you figure out where you wanted to go eat?" Dad asked.

I shook my head. "I was thinking that sushi place, but I'm not sure if anyone likes it like I do."

"I like sushi!" Hancock called, interrupting his interview to tell us that little tidbit.

"But I don't like sushi from that one place. So, avoid that please!" Teller followed up.

Shaking my head, I returned my eyes back to my mom.

Pitch Please

"We're gonna have to nix sushi," I informed them.

"I noticed," Mom smiled. "There's that new place, Across the Border."

"It's *On The Border*, dear, and that place just opened. They'll be busy as hell," Dad interrupted.

Mom sighed.

"I just don't understand why you don't like Mexican food. It's the best food in the world," Mom started in with her usual argument, which caused my father to follow up with his usual argument.

"What I really want is a hamburger," Hancock said, interrupting my parents. "But I can do sushi."

Hancock's arm went around my hips where I was leaning against the padded wall, and he pulled me in tight while his eyes went to my parents.

"Nice to meet you," he offered my father his hand.

Dad took it, considering the man in front of him, while my mother continued her argument about the pros and cons of her favorite cuisine.

"Nice to meet you, too," Dad replied, dropping his hand.

"Mexican food has queso. And tortilla chips. And beans. Oh, and sizzling fajita meat."

"We're not doing sushi," I said firmly. "You just said you liked sushi on national television. Every fan in Longview will now be patrolling all the sushi places in the area looking for you. We can do hamburgers."

Hancock frowned. "I didn't say we were going to a sushi place."

"No," I nodded. "But why else would you say you like sushi in the middle of an interview?"

The sweetness in my voice was enough to cause Hancock's eyes to narrow.

"Wow," he teased. "That tongue of yours has gotten sharp over the last two weeks."

My mouth kicked up in a smile.

"I thought you liked my…"

He pressed one large palm over my mouth and glared at me.

"Your parents…whom I'm trying to impress…are right there. Enough of that," he whispered into my ear.

But he hadn't said it softly enough.

"Oh, you've already impressed us," my mom smiled. "Those home runs…those were works of art."

"Hey, what am I, chopped liver?" Teller patted his chest.

I threw myself in Teller's direction and started peppering his face with kisses.

"What's wrong, Telly Belly?" I squeezed his neck as hard as I could. "Is somebody a sore loser?"

My brother let this happen for all of five seconds before he slipped away.

"Must you always embarrass me?" he whined, replacing his hat to the correct angle and glaring at me while he did it.

"Yes," I said. "It's my job as an older sister," I informed him. "You know this."

"Yeah," he brushed off some invisible lint. "But I'm a professional now. This isn't me playing little league anymore."

My eyes gleamed.

"I could always make it worse."

His eyes widened. "Don't you dare."

"Food, children," my dad groaned. "Can't we just go get food? It's already nine o'clock, and I'm literally wasting away over here."

"You had three hot dogs and two beers during the game," I pointed out. "I watched you."

My dad shrugged.

"That doesn't mean that I'm not still hungry," he grumbled.

"Do you mind if I bring a couple of friends?" Hancock asked my parents.

"Absolutely not. Bring as many friends as you want," my mother and father said at the same time. "And call us Jester and Melanie."

Hancock's lip twitched. "I can do that. Can y'all give me thirty minutes to get ready?"

"I need that, too. Gotta get my shit packed up, and I can meet y'all in the lot," Teller confirmed.

"Nobody cares about you," I told Teller. "And, in fact, nobody invited you."

Teller shrugged. "Wait for me, Mom!"

I rolled my eyes as I grabbed Hancock's hand. He was watching us bicker back and forth like we were an amusing reality TV show that he was being sucked into.

"Come on," I pulled his arm. "Or we're going to be late."

"Why would we be late?" he asked as we made our way down the tunnel that led to the offices, as well as the locker room.

The moment we got to my office door, I opened it and dragged Hancock inside.

Hancock's face was amused as I slammed the door, but that look quickly fell away as he watched me strip my pants down my hips.

"I delegated," I informed him. "Everyone's taking care of their players. Now it's time to take care of mine."

His eyes widened even further.

Then something seemed to snap, and he started to strip his pants down his legs all the while still trying to hold his hat and glove.

Once he realized he wasn't going to get it undone without dropping it, everything went to the floor.

I kicked my pants off and then started on my shirt.

It was when I was struggling to get to my bra that Hancock lifted me directly underneath my ass and pinned me to the wall.

"Hancock!" I cried out. "Put me down before you break your back."

He didn't bother replying as he buried his face against my breasts.

"I've missed you," he whispered fervently.

"Me or my breasts?" I gasped as he sucked one peaked nipple into his mouth.

"Your breasts."

He didn't even bother to lie.

That was the type of man Hancock was.

"But what about me?" I gasped as his hard cock pressed up against my pussy. "Did you miss anything more than my breasts?"

He ground his cock into my clit, and I closed my eyes in reaction.

"I missed a lot of things," he said around my nipple. "For instance," he let one hand drop until it was at his cock, which he aimed at my pussy. "I've missed this tight, hot thing right here."

He pushed inside of me, allowing the arm wrapped around my waist to loosen so gravity could do the work.

And it did. Well.

I sank slowly on his cock and gasped when he bottomed out inside of me.

"I've missed holding you in my arms." He kissed my lips. "I've missed listening to you talk in your sleep."

"I don't talk in my sleep!" I cried out.

"I missed the way you talked to Ruby—which proves that you think she's as smart as I do."

I didn't bother to refute that one. I'd been doing nothing but talking to her for the last two weeks. I talked to her like she was my roommate instead of my boyfriend's dog.

"I missed the way you enjoy your food, and the way you moan when you taste something sweet." He thrust forward, making my body jolt. "And I missed the way you brush your teeth. The way you let the toothpaste run down your chin, making you look like you're foaming at the mouth."

I started to giggle.

"But mostly…mostly, I missed you. Your face. Your breath on my shoulder as we watched a movie. The way you felt in my arms. The way you smelled. Everything that's you, I missed."

I freakin' melted.

If he hadn't already had me up against the wall, I would've collapsed to the floor in a puddle of lovesick goo.

Leaning forward so our lips were only a hairsbreadth away, I whispered to him. Told him exactly what I felt, too.

"I slept with your dog, and we kept each other company. We were both miserable without you," I informed him. "We didn't wash the sheets yet, either. I'm scared to see what Ruby's side of the bed looks like."

He threw his head back and laughed.

And his laughter caused his dick to jump inside of me, making me moan in response.

"I'm glad," he teased. "Now give me your mouth while I fuck you."

I gave him my mouth.

I also gave him a hickey and scratched his back and chest up in my excitement.

Between one breath and the next, all of our banter was gone, and what was left was quiet breathing and soft sighs.

"Please," I whispered as he pulled his cock out of me completely. "Why are you stopping?"

I was trying to be quiet.

We were in my office, yes, but we weren't alone in the building.

In fact, I knew for certain there were still people in the training room because I could hear them talking.

Which was why I wasn't screaming at Hancock to 'fuck me' or 'take me harder' like I really wanted to.

Without waiting for me to come to my senses, he pulled me away from the wall, turned me around, and shoved me over the folding chair that was at the end of my desk. The one that was cold and metal. The one that screeched in protest when I put my feet on it after a long, hard day.

The one that everyone would hear if it collapsed under my weight.

But before I could sound the alarm, Hancock filled me once again.

To the brim.

There wasn't a single millimeter of space inside of me that he wasn't currently filling with his cock.

And I found myself without air as I tried to make sense of what was going on.

But just as quickly as he filled me, he pulled back out.

There was no wasting time anymore, though.

He continuously pulled out only to shove home, causing not only the chair to squeak across the tiled floor of my office, but also my breasts to bounce against the metal back of the chair.

The slap-slap-screech was probably heard in all corners of the entire freakin' floor, but I couldn't find it in me to care.

Not when I was on the brink of orgasm.

Slap-slap-screech.

"Shhhiiiit."

I closed my eyes and immediately dropped my hand between my legs, finishing before he could slow to a stop.

Because I knew what that word meant.

He'd lost control.

And if I wanted to come with him, or at all, I would be doing it on my own.

Not because he wasn't the type of man that would take care of me, but because I wanted to come with him instead of afterwards.

I wanted to feel his heat inside of me, filling me, as my orgasm took me over.

And that's exactly what happened.

The moment my pussy started to ripple around him, he grunted and his come started to pulse into me.

His cock jerked each time my pussy clamped down, and both of us groaned as our releases took us over.

"Yo!" Someone knocked on our door. "Y'all better not be fucking in there while I'm waiting to eat. It's been eight goddamned hours. You know I don't eat before the game, Sway Bar!"

"What the hell?" Hancock stood up. "Why is he calling you Sway Bar?"

"Because he's stupid," I mumbled, pushing up so the metal chair wasn't digging uncomfortably into the middle of my chest.

"I think your brother just caught us having sex. Dammit, I wanted him to like me," Hancock muttered darkly.

I snorted and pushed myself all the way up, then did the waddle-sex-walk back to my desk where I kept my wipes when I had food mishaps.

They were the scented kind that smelled like flowers since I couldn't stand the regular baby powder smell—meaning my coochie would smell like it too.

But it wasn't something I could control. So, I would have a flowery vagina—which wasn't necessarily a bad thing—but the scent was so strong that I would be smelling it for the rest of the night.

"This is terrible," Hancock muttered to himself some more. "Do you think he'll tell your parents?"

I ignored him and cleaned myself up, then walked over to my panties and grimaced.

They were wet. Both from sweat due to sitting in a hot dugout for three hours, and from my need for Hancock.

But they'd have to do, because I sure as hell wasn't going to be wearing nothing underneath the most uncomfortable pants in the world that the Lumberjack staff forced me to wear while at home games.

They were these tight—non-stretch—pants that had absolutely no give to them. They dug uncomfortably into my sides, giving me the appearance of more love handles than I actually had.

"I think it'll be okay," Hancock continued. "I feel like I'm going to have a heart attack."

I rolled my eyes and let him continue his freak out, then did the shimmy shake into my khaki pants.

"You might want to get dressed," I mentioned. "Or you'll be late—which *will* give them cause to be upset."

He shut up almost instantly, slid on his pants and nothing else, and then left the room without another word.

Giggling, I was just picking up my shirt when a knock sounded at the door.

But instead of whomever it was waiting to get permission, they just walked right in.

"Listen, Sway," Sinclair was saying before he'd even looked up. "Croft is having some lower groin issues that I think you should take a look…"

He stopped as I hastily yanked my shirt down over my breasts. My unbound breasts.

"Get out!" I screamed. "And it's customary to freakin' wait for a knock to be answered before you just come busting in!"

"Well, Hancock just came out— so I assumed you were done checking his groin for injuries," he sneered. "It's only fair that you check Croft, too."

I narrowed my eyes.

"Get out," I snapped. "And it's your job as my assistant to take care of the non-starters. Always has been, always will be. Now get out."

Normally, I would've looked at it.

I did not care who started and who didn't. I treated them all equally. Croft, however, gave me the creeps. He also tried to come on to me more than once while Hancock was away. Normally, that would be fine, I could handle it. I had handled it from other players and staff before.

However, this time, Croft had seriously squigged me out.

So much so that I was glad I was staying at Hancock's place that had security in the form of an alarm and a big, bad half-breed Husky to protect me.

Sinclair's eyes went to my unbound breasts behind my t-shirt, and I was just about to tell him to get out again when a hand flashed into the room, gripped Sinclair around the neck, and yanked him back out of the room.

The smile that lit my face was likely a mean one, but there was nothing for it.

Hancock was a freakin' dream come true. He was everything and anything I could've ever asked for.

He protected me even when I didn't realize I needed protecting.

"Thank you!" I called out. "I'll be out in just a few minutes so we can leave!"

"You're welcome," came Hancock's gruff reply.

***

"I think your parents like me," Hancock mumbled as he curled into me. "Do you think they liked me?"

I sighed.

"They loved you, Hancock. Or they would've never invited you to their place," I informed him for the fifth time. "Promise. Now go to sleep."

He rolled so he was on top of me.

"What if I didn't want to go to sleep?" he asked, wiggling his big body until he fell between my thighs.

I lifted my hips to grind my unclothed nether regions into his thickening cock and raised my brows. "What did you have in mind?"

His mouth lifted at the corner, and then he took my hands and pinned them above my head.

"I guess I'll have to show you."

And he showed me. Multiple times throughout the night.

Sleep was overrated anyway.

***

"Tell me what happened."

He shook his head. "I don't want to talk about it right now. Right now, I just want to hold you."

"But you'll tell me?"

He nodded. "When I can."

And I gave him that, because that's what happened when the man you loved asked for more time.

CHAPTER 23

Masturbation is a form of stress relief. So, go fuck yourself and check the bitch at the door next time you visit.
-Hancock's secret thoughts

Hancock

"Can we help?" I called to the woman who was stalled in the middle of the road.

Gentry stopped next to me, panting heavily, just like me, from our run, and stared at the lady with concern.

The woman started to cry.

"That would be wonderful," she wiped her tears. "My son is in the backseat, and I've been trying to get out, but every time I do, a car whizzes by."

We were on a main road in the busiest part of Longview, during rush hour, when everyone drove like assholes to get home.

So yeah, I could understand her hesitation to get out of the vehicle.

"Put it in neutral," I hollered. "And keep your foot off the break!"

Once we were sure we weren't going to be run over—because that would be a lot fun to explain to our coach—Gentry and I got behind the SUV and started to push.

Gentry cursed, and I looked over at him to see him shaking out his left hand while he pushed with his shoulder and right hand.

"What?" I asked, straining.

The SUV started to roll slowly forward, but eventually started to gain speed giving us a small break, and I grunted.

"Jesus, it feels like there are bricks in this thing," Gentry grumbled, sweat pouring even more heavily down his face.

I looked up in time to see the parking lot ahead, and I yelled out over the din of traffic.

"Turn the wheel!"

She turned the wheel, and we managed to push it the last few feet into the parking lot before it stopped completely.

"Damn," Gentry said, backing away.

The woman hurried out of the SUV, and she ran to the back hatch where we were leaning heavily.

"Oh, God," she said the moment she was back there. "Is your hand okay?"

My eyes immediately went to Gentry's hand, and I breathed a sigh of relief when I saw it wasn't his pitching hand.

"Yeah, fine," he grumbled, starting to press it to his shirt to stop the bleeding.

"Wait!" she cried. "I have some Band-Aids in the car."

She hurried around the other side of the SUV, and came back moments later with a little red pack in her hands.

"I carry this everywhere. I hope you like Transformer Band-Aids," she smiled timidly.

Gentry held out his hand, which she reached for, and she pressed a white gauze pad against it before covering it with the Band-Aid.

"Bumblebee," Gentry murmured. "My favorite."

The woman started to laugh.

"You and Cailean," she pointed to the back seat where I assumed her son was sitting.

Gentry looked through the glass, and his eyes widened.

"You're not kidding."

The woman shook her head.

"No, I'm afraid I'm not," she grinned.

I took a look myself and smiled when I saw the kid fully decked out in Transformer clothes—Bumblebee to be exact—and waving at us.

"Happy kid," I mumbled.

"He thought it was fun," she sighed. "Now I have to go beg my dad for a ride."

"You sound like you'd rather saw off your own foot," Gentry observed.

"I would," she confirmed. "My dad's a mechanic, and I'd rather not hear him say 'I told you so' about buying this car."

"Why?" Gentry asked. "What's wrong with it?"

She grinned.

"It's not American made."

Gentry and I both nodded, understanding clear now.

"He a soldier?" I wondered.

She nodded her head again.

"Army. Retired after twenty years," she confirmed.

"Well, we'll wait until someone comes. As long as you're comfortable with that," Gentry offered.

The woman looked relieved.

"Thank you," she whispered, and then pulled out her phone, a look of pain on her face. "I'll be biting the bullet over there for a few seconds."

With that, she walked away, and I looked over at my still staring friend.

"You might want to wipe that drool off your face."

Gentry's head whipped around to stare at me.

"Fuck off."

***

"That little fucker is about to have his ass handed to him," I murmured to Gentry as we walked into the locker room half an hour later. "What's his deal?"

Gentry's eyes went to the kid in question.

Croft was shoving his shirt into his pants, making sure he was tucked in completely all the way around his body, before he turned to grab his glove.

A glove that looked exactly like mine, even down to the red nail polish on the tip of the left finger.

That was something my mother used to do to all of our gloves as a way to distinguish my glove from all of my brothers. I had red. Hannibal had green. Hunter had blue. Harrison had orange. And Holden had yellow.

Which made me wonder...why the hell did that kid have a glove with red tipped fingers? Nobody else did that, and I began to ponder the likelihood of him doing the same thing with the red paint. It wasn't a fucking coincidence that that kid had it and I did, too.

Which got me to thinking.

I hated the glove.

There was something wrong with it since I'd gotten it back, and I didn't like it one freakin' bit.

"What's wrong?" Gentry pushed.

"Fuckin' glove has felt off since I got it back," I grumbled. "Gonna have to switch to my back up."

"You should start breaking in a new one," Gentry suggested.

I sighed.

"I am, and I will," I mumbled. "How's your hand doing?"

"Fine," he murmured. "Better since I got the Band-Aid, unbelievably."

I snorted and hunched my shoulders as I ripped my shirt over my head, throwing it in the bag at the bottom of my locker.

"Do you think she'll come to the game next week?" I questioned him.

He'd invited her to the game when he'd seen her face after she'd spoken with her dad, and her eyes had gone all round as she looked from me to Gentry.

"Yeah," Gentry nodded his head. "I do believe that she will."

Turning my smile away from him so he wouldn't see it, I bent down and grabbed a clean shirt just as I heard Rhys clear his throat directly next to me.

I turned only my head and raised a brow at him. "Can I help you?"

"You might want to head to the training room," he mentioned. "Stop right outside the door."

Brows furrowed, I did just that, leaving my clean t-shirt on the bench behind my locker as I weaved my way through the people milling about here and there as they trickled in from their workouts.

At first, I wasn't too concerned.

Rhys looked fairly calm.

Nothing could be too wrong with Sway if he was that calm, right?

Wrong.

I realized about thirty seconds after arriving at the doors to the training room why he'd been so calm.

He didn't want to say anything and risk taking the brunt of my anger. So, he'd sent me here, knowing I would hear.

"Look at her trying to lift that box of supplies. Seriously. How hard is it to lift forty pounds? I had to sign a sheet saying that I could lift up to sixty pounds to even get signed on," another trainer I didn't know very well said.

"She's a fat ass," I heard Sinclair snap. "Sway can't even do the most basic tasks. How is she still allowed to work here?"

"Excuse me? She's my fat ass," I heard myself saying. "Now get the fuck out. You won't be working here in an hour. You might want to go ahead and pack your stuff."

Sway turned the moment she heard my voice, and then her eyes narrowed at what had come out of my mouth.

But I had no time to soothe the hurt I saw on her face.

Not when I was this fucking mad.

"You have no authority to get me fired," Sinclair snapped. "Now if you'll excuse me."

"Siggy!" I bellowed.

Siggy, who I'd seen in his office on my way to the training room, came barreling out of his office like he'd been shot from a cannon.

"What's wrong?" he asked, jogging over toward me.

"Your assistant trainer just called my woman a fat ass."

Sway gasped, as did everyone else in the room.

I hadn't actually claimed her publicly before, and that showed on her face, making me realize what an incredible shithead I'd been for not doing it before now.

"Since when is she your woman?" Gentry teased from behind me.

"Since a couple of weeks ago," I answered quickly. "Now shut up, and go get your hand looked at."

"I'll do it," Sway volunteered, her eyes going wildly around the room.

I nodded. "Thank you, baby."

Everyone stayed quiet until Gentry and Sway had left the training room.

"Sinclair," Siggy started. "I suggest you pack your office up now. You won't be working here by tomorrow afternoon."

"You can't fire me," Sinclair snapped.

"*I* can't, no." Siggy agreed. "But I can suggest it to the people who can, and trust me, I *will* be doing that. If I can't trust you to treat Sway correctly, how can I trust you to treat my players?" Siggy paused. "And honestly, Sway could fire you right now, seeing as she's your superior. The question is, why hasn't she?"

Sinclair's eyes narrowed.

"I've worked here for four years now. They're not going to fire me because of one insignificant comment," Sinclair snapped, looking wildly around the room now for support.

"An insignificant comment that you made about the coach's niece and the girlfriend of Hancock Peters," someone muttered.

Sinclair's mouth twisted in fury at hearing that comment.

"We're not allowed to fraternize with the players. This…" he gestured to me and where Sway had disappeared into her office. "This isn't even allowed. How, and why, she should get special treatment doesn't even compute in my brain."

"Maybe it's because your brain is malfunctioning," I murmured, crossing my arms tightly over my chest. "Never once, in my years of life, have I seen someone act so uncaring to another human being. You need to rethink your choices and start acting like a decent human being to people who don't fit into your nice, perfect little box."

"She disgusts me," Sinclair sneered.

"That woman is the most beautiful person in this whole entire world. She makes my heart skip beats when I look at her across my pillow in the morning." I cleared my throat. "I'm lucky to have her as my girlfriend. I'm lucky to have her as my friend…and you would have been her friend as well had you treated her with the respect she deserves. Now you'll never know and not because she wouldn't forgive you if you worked for that forgiveness, but because I won't let you near her again. You'll never get the chance to apologize, and I can't find it in me to care."

His eyes settled on Croft, who was busy looking between me, Siggy and Sinclair before starting the cycle completely over again.

"Say something," Sinclair demanded of Croft.

Croft's mouth opened and then closed.

When nothing came forth, Sinclair's eyes narrowed.

"You'll regret this," Sinclair promised. "You should be careful who you share your discrepancies with."

With that, Sinclair left, not bothering to clean his office out.

It was obvious that he thought he'd be back.

If I had my way, though, he wouldn't. Not now, and not ever.

Siggy and I watched him go, as did about five other players, including Rhys.

"Thank you," I said to the man who'd told me about the situation in the first place. "I appreciate it."

Rhys shrugged. "You'd have done the same had the situation been reversed."

"Now I have to go apologize for calling my woman names when I really didn't mean what came out."

"I hope you meant some of them," Sway replied from behind me.

I turned.

And then the words started to fall out of my mouth without me being able to control them.

"The words…they came out wrong," I apologized. "I swear. I don't think you're a fat ass. In fact, I think you're beautiful. I think you're perfect. I love your curves, and the way they cup my hardness. I love the way you feel when I lay next to you. I swear, I didn't really mean those ugly words." I promised her.

"Did you mean it?" she asked.

I blinked, surprised by her understanding tone.

"Mean what?" I asked, confused.

She smiled. "That I make your heart race."

I pulled her hand to my body, and flattened it against where my heart was thundering in my chest.

"Does that answer your question?" I asked.

She smiled.

"I love you, Hancock." She threw her arms around my neck. "Now it's time to get you dressed so we can go to the house for a few. We have dinner with your friends in a few short hours, and I forgot something at your place."

My brows furrowed.

"That's three hours from now," I said. "What did you forget?"

She leaned forward, her lips deliberately brushing against my ear, and her whispered words had the power to make my heart hammer.

I'm starting to forget what it feels like to have you inside of me.

***

"Do you remember yet?" I asked, thrusting so hard into her that her breasts jumped.

She arched her back, her eyes closing.

"No." She shook her head. "Fuck me harder, it might come back to me."

I grinned and did just that.

CHAPTER 24

I just like baseball. Baseball's my favorite.
-Sway's secret thoughts

Sway

81st game of the season
Texas Lumberjacks v. San Diego Devildogs
Home Game

My eyes widened when I saw the sheer amount of man flesh around the table where we were seated.

They'd been the same way at dinner last night. Intimidating. Handsome. Strong. Silent.

Definitely a lot more strong and silent than I was sure they were used to being.

Today they were a little more outgoing, but their eyes scanned the restaurant around us like they were waiting for the doors to open and bad guys to start pouring in.

Especially Hancock's brother, Hannibal.

Hannibal's entire body was twitching and flinching each time a loud noise sounded around us.

Acting like I didn't notice the fourth time he jumped in the last three minutes, I held out my phone to him.

"I took a picture of your brother last night that I thought you might like," I showed him, hitting the home button on my phone.

The phone's screen lit up, and I had to stop myself from laughing.

Again.

"Ruby was supposed to be mine, but I was deployed when she was about seven weeks old. So, I just gave her to him. Looks like I made a good choice," Hannibal observed.

I grinned.

"I'm not actually sure how she got up there, or what was funnier. Her attempting to get down when she saw him, or him trying to climb up there to get her, scared that if he didn't go after her she'd fall over the edge," I told him.

The photo was of Ruby in one of the many weird places that she has gotten herself into since I'd been in her life, but this one was definitely the most adventurous and unusual.

"Let me see," another man—I thought his name was Tucker—ordered.

And it was an order.

It definitely wasn't a request.

I showed him anyway, though.

"Wow," Tucker said in surprise. "How did she get up there?"

I grinned, bringing the picture back to look at it.

"Well, we think she jumped up on the grill, and then walked along the deck railing like a balance beam to the awning, which she jumped up on," I murmured. "Do you think you'll get another dog?"

Hannibal looked at me, his eyes so much like the ones I loved, that it startled me for a long second.

"Yes," he agreed. "Once I decide if I'm done doing what I'm doing, that is."

My smile was small.

"Your brother was hoping that would be sooner rather than later," I murmured.

Hannibal shrugged.

"It likely will be," he mumbled. "Though it'll probably take a bullet bringing me down permanently to make me see reason."

My heart rate sped up.

"Almost bit it before my brother had to come and rescue me," he continued speaking, almost as if he wasn't even aware of what he was saying.

His eyes were focused on something in the distance, and definitely not the Japanese hibachi chef right in front of us, frying up the rice for our meal.

"Never thought my brother could take a life like he did."

My belly somersaulted.

He'd taken a life?

I didn't dare interrupt him, though, in the hopes that he would continue instead of stopping once he realized who he was talking to.

"Looked up, saw all my boys around me…and there was my brother, a gun in his hand, and his heart in his eyes," he sighed. "Jesus Christ. The man is worth millions, and he came out there to save my ass? Do you have any idea what would've happened if he'd died over there?"

No. No, I didn't.

"But my brother showed his face around town. Got some people scared. And they started to scramble," he sighed. "Knew it the day that they first spotted him. Had my captors come and check on me every single hour on the hour. Then there was a lot of chattering about them killing me off to save themselves the headache, but the big guy…he didn't want to kill me right away. He wanted to do it publicly, on a day that was significant to the US."

My belly rolled.

"It would've been bad if he didn't come."

That wasn't news to me.

I'd gotten the same feeling from Leslie when he'd explained the mechanics of it.

Now I just wondered if the people responsible were caught, or if I had to continue to worry about Hannibal.

But Hannibal answered my question without realizing I'd wanted to know the details.

"They found the leak in the chain of command and fired him. Now he'll probably spend the rest of his life in a place like the hellhole where I was held captive in for three weeks," Hannibal spoke.

"What are y'all whispering about over here?" Tucker—now I was sure that was him—asked as he took a seat next to Hannibal, his eyes on my face that I was sure was white as a ghost.

"We're talking about how the Lumberjacks won tonight," I continued, lying through my teeth. "And what that means for their chances at making the playoffs."

"Let's not talk about this," one of the men, Tim Teague, the leader of this band of misfits, groaned. "That's all we heard about the entire time we were with this joker."

He pointed to a bashful looking Hancock, who was staring at his hands like he was about to strangle Tim.

The rest of the group laughed, as did Hannibal.

"They hate it," Hannibal added. "I made them watch the games, even though they couldn't stand watching the Lumberjacks. But since I forced them, they've become unwilling fans."

"We got rid of you and then your brother shows up, forcing us to watch the same shit. It was like you were still there," Park grumbled.

Instead of the blow up I expected, it only caused relieved chuckles all the way around, and I wondered if this was some weird way that they relieved stress.

"Where are you from, Park?" I reached out for my drink and brought it to my lips. "You sound like you have a southern twang to your speech."

He grimaced. "Florida."

"Do you have any family there?"

Another darker grimace rolled over Park's face.

"What Park isn't telling you is that he was a gang banger when he was younger, so he has family, just not any that likes him," Hannibal added when he was sure that Park wasn't going to say anything on the subject matter.

My mouth dropped open.

Was he being serious?

But I could tell by the death glare that Park was sending Hannibal that he was being very serious.

"That's…uhhh…interesting," I finally added. "Is that where you got the tattoos?"

I pointed to the tattoos that lined his arms.

Hancock had tattoos. As did most of these men.

But Park's were darker.

Scarier and more crude looking.

"Yeah," he said. "Most of 'em I got before I was seventeen." He held up his hands and rotated his arms, his big muscles bulging each time he moved.

"What about the one on your neck?" I pointed to one that looked like a single black line that ran completely around his neck, just below his Adam's apple.

Park's face closed off, and instantly I knew he wouldn't be answering that.

As did the rest of them if the look on their faces was anything to go by.

"Do you have seats for us tomorrow?" Hannibal asked his brother. "We're in town for another thirty-six hours, and that's enough to take in a game."

Hancock's lips twitched with the knowledge that these boys were going to be forced to watch a game in real time. "Yeah, I can get some next to mom and dad."

Hannibal grimaced.

"I'm not getting out of seeing them, am I?" he asked.

Hancock shook his head. "No, I don't think you are."

"Fucking wonderful."

***

"I'm late, I'm late, for a very important date…" I chattered as I hurried to the door that would lead me into the stadium.

Soren, the guard who was posted at the back entrance at every home game, waved at me and opened the door.

"How are you, Miss Sway?" he asked politely.

"I'm great, Soren. How are you?" I returned sweetly as I passed.

"Two more weeks!" he informed me. "That means I'm freakin' great."

I started to chuckle.

Soren and his wife were having their first child together, and she'd been on bed rest since she was seventeen weeks pregnant. Now at thirty-five weeks, she only had two more weeks until she was allowed to move about.

"That's wonderful news!" I told him sincerely. "It'll be here before you know it, and you'll have your sleepless nights to deal with!"

He chuckled as he waved me on, and I started for the stairs.

I looked down at the new Fitbit on my hand, the one Hancock had given to me the night before.

He'd received it as part of a promotional campaign, and he was supposed to wear it and then let them know what he thought of the product.

Except Hancock didn't wear anything on his wrists during games or practices—which happened to be what he was doing much of the time during the season—so he'd given it to me.

It was cool, I'd give them that.

It was also motivating.

I hadn't realized how little I moved until this thing on my wrist told me.

Which, I suppose, was the whole purpose of this product in the first place.

Normally, I would've taken the elevator to where I needed to go, but today I chose the stairs to boost today's step count hit since yesterdays had been so pitifully lame.

I'd just crested the first flight of stairs when I saw Sinclair coming down from the flight above me, a box in his hands and a scowl on his face.

"Fuckin' bitch," Sinclair growled. "This is all your fault."

At first, I thought he was talking to me, but it soon became apparent that he wasn't when he looked over his shoulder.

"Not sure why you think it's my fault," Croft grumbled. "I paid you kindly for what you did."

"Not kindly enough to lose this job. Do you realize how much I make a year?" he asked. "Two hundred K. That's twice the amount that you offered to pay me for doing your dirty work."

"You did this to yourself. I paid you. I never told you to make friends with that bitch's ex-boyfriend or try to get her fired," Croft shot back. "That's all on you."

"Well you better find a way to get me another decent-paying job, or I'll let everyone know that you were the one stealing everybody's stuff," Sinclair snapped.

"It wasn't stealing. I borrowed," Croft replied.

"You stole the glove. You made a copy of the glove, but you still have the original," Sinclair stopped and dropped his box to the stairs. "You took Manny's bubble gum and Jessup's batting gloves."

"You don't know what you're talking about," Croft narrowed his eyes.

"I do know what I'm talking about." Sinclair crossed his arms over his chest. "And that'll get you kicked out of this place just as surely as calling that bitch a fat ass will."

I went to the landing and tried the door handle, thankful that it wasn't locked.

It led to the locker room level, which usually was locked.

Luckily, not today, because without waiting for a reply, Sinclair picked his box up and tucked it under his arm.

"I suggest you figure out whether having a professional baseball career is worth…you fucking bitch!"

This time I knew he was talking to me. I knew it, mostly because the moment I tried to go into the door, someone was coming out of it, forcing me to back up whether I wanted to or not.

"Language," the big man, Furious George, replied. "Sorry, little lady. Did you need something in here?"

I nodded my head and then blushed.

I didn't normally go into the locker room if there was a possibility that they were getting dressed, if I could help it. Most of them walked around naked half the time, and if I could save myself the embarrassment of seeing men who weren't Hancock naked, I'd do it.

"I was trying to see Hancock," I lied. "Is he in there?"

Furious George's face went from me, to the stairs above me where I suspected Sinclair and Croft were standing, glaring most likely.

"How about you and me walk up there together?" he asked. "I wanted to get you to look at my wrist anyway. I had to play with a different bat yesterday because mine went missing, and now it's killing me."

I wanted to scream at Croft, asking him if he'd stolen George's bat, too, but I managed to control that reaction.

But just barely.

I could tell when we passed Croft that he knew I was about to blab everything.

Which was why, in the next moment, he grabbed me by the hair as I moved by him and tried to throw me down the stairs.

But suddenly we weren't alone.

George took Croft by the throat as I started to fall.

Or would have fallen had my man not caught me before I could go tumbling down the stairs.

"Jesus fucking Christ!" Hancock hissed, pulling me protectively into his arms and burying his face into my neck. "What the hell is wrong with that fucking kid?"

George's hand tightened on the kid's throat, and Sinclair took in the look on both George and Hancock's faces and decided to cut his losses.

Without another word, he left, leaving us alone with a purple-faced Croft who had a whole lot of questions to answer.

His interrogation took about an hour as Siggy got into drill sergeant mode— something he'd picked up during his eight years in the Army— and grilled Croft until he confessed to every single thing he'd stolen over the course of the season.

Something I wasn't able to stay and witness since I had a whole baseball team to prepare for the upcoming game, and two assistants, who could only work under my direction since they weren't certified athletic trainers like I was.

Forty-five minutes later, I was bending over to check my bag that I took with me to all the games when I felt someone come up behind me.

I knew it was Hancock without even looking up.

Not because I could smell him or feel him, but because he was just that big of a presence. It was like my body was tuned in to his, and I knew it was him from the electrical charge I always felt when he was close.

"You ready, big boy?" I asked him.

He stilled my hips that I didn't even realize were swaying to the music playing softly on the phone in my pocket and fitted his chest against my back.

"I'm ready," he agreed. "Even more ready now that I have my glove back."

"You have your glove back?" I whispered, straightening. "But I didn't even tell you that..."

"I heard everything that was said. I'd already come into the stairwell to meet you in the parking lot, but I froze when I heard Sinclair and Croft talking," he explained. "That's why I was late getting to you."

I harrumphed.

"I can't believe that kid stole all those things." I shook my head in confusion. "From what I understand, he was a decent catcher at one time. He didn't need to steal y'all's shit to get any better."

"My guess is that the kid just wanted to fit in. Maybe he wanted to commiserate with the players that lost something," he explained. "But we won't know for sure until Siggy gets done with him."

I shuddered as I thought about Siggy getting done with him.

"Alright, you handsome man, are you ready to play?" I asked, changing the subject to something a little less sad.

My handsome man with his badass beard smiled.

"I will be as soon as you give me my kiss."

I gave him a kiss.

"Break a leg."

His eyes crossed.

"That's not what you're supposed to say!" he growled in exasperation. "Never!"

I rolled my eyes.

"Then what am I supposed to say?" I questioned.

"Have a good game?" he tried. "Telling me to break a leg isn't something you'd ever want to wish on me."

"Whatever."

"Not whatever," he countered. "If I break a leg, you're going to regret it."

"You won't break a leg. Now get out there, and show 'em what you got." I shouldered my bag. "I'll see you on the bench."

He sighed and pushed away, holding my office door open for me.

"Yes, ma'am."

It was in the second inning that he broke a leg.

Luckily, it wasn't *his* own leg that he broke, but the other team's catcher's leg when he had tried to stop Hancock from crossing home plate.

He scored, and the catcher got a season-ending injury for his efforts.

CHAPTER 25

Catcher has a big butt.
-Things you shouldn't say to your boyfriend/professional baseball player that just so happens to be a catcher.

Hancock

162nd game of the season
Texas Lumberjacks v. Shreveport Sparks
Home Game

"Good to see you," I offered my hand to the man who was sitting along the first base line, Gabe. "How's it going."

Ember took my hand as well and then gestured to the perky blonde next to her. "This is Rainie."

Rainie waved spastically, and I decided these two ladies in front of me were perfect for my Sway.

"You know what to do?" I asked.

Rainie and Ember both nodded.

"We do," both women promised.

I grinned and handed the man, Gabe, my ring box.

"I would give it to my mom, but she wouldn't be able to hold it in…and my brothers are three sheets to the wind." I pointed at my brothers and parents who were sitting just above the dugout.

"That's pretty funny, actually," Ember giggled. "Hannibal was just telling us how much your mom drives him crazy."

I grinned, my eyes straying over to my brother. He was miserable right now.

After careful consideration, he'd decided to take a hiatus from the black ops team—a hiatus that his CO insisted on for his 'mental health.' Though the reason behind this break wasn't a good one, I could see my brother getting better daily.

Although I was sure that had a lot to do with him doing hard, manual labor at our family's ranch—a place we were headed to this evening after the game for a fun-filled weekend of branding the new cattle.

I still helped around the ranch when I had time, and since this was the last game of the season, it coincided perfectly with the ranch. Which meant my parents wouldn't have to hire anybody to help since not only was I coming to help, but Hannibal was there now, too.

"She's worried about her baby," I teased. "He's the last one who hasn't found someone, and she wants to make sure he's not alone forever."

Ember snorted.

"He went with us to The Back Porch yesterday. He had no trouble finding women," Ember pointed out.

"No," I agreed. "He's never had that problem. What she's worried about is him finding someone who'll be good enough for her to get some grandbabies from."

"Ahhh," Ember nodded.

"She should probably start checking out Longview, then," Gabe grinned. "All the good ones are taken in Kilgore."

Ember smacked her husband's chest.

"That's not true," she disagreed. "There's that girl at the supermarket…and our son's teacher."

Gabe's eyes sparkled. "You want to set up poor, sweet, innocent Hannibal with that harpy who teaches Luca? You've got to be kidding."

Chuckling, I waved them off and headed for the dugout where my woman had just taken her seat.

In my spot.

"You're in my seat!" I bellowed the moment I was at the top of the steps.

Sway didn't bother to look up.

"Imagine that," she mused. "I sure am."

Hooking her around the waist with one arm, I scooted her down and took my place directly beside her.

"You forgot to kiss me," I declared.

She offered her lips, but kept her eyes on the book that she was reading. One with a jacked guy in a kilt on the cover.

"Good book?" I asked, her, waiting for her to look into my eyes.

"Great book," she nodded. "Are you going to kiss me or what?"

I gave her a kiss.

"Now what do you say?" I teased.

"Break…" I pressed my hand over her mouth before she could finish that thought.

"Sway," I glared.

She grinned broadly behind my hand. So widely, in fact, I could feel her teeth on my fingers.

"I hope you have a good game and hit two home runs," she said sweetly.

I sighed.

"I guess that's good enough."

"And now if everyone will please stand for the National Anthem."

I touched the tip of Sway's nose with my pointer finger, and then climbed the steps to take my spot on the field with my hand over my heart.

Furious George came up to me and slapped me on the back before following suit.

"The kid wanted me to thank you again for coming to see him at the hospital yesterday," George murmured. "He said you brought signed baseballs for the entire floor. Are you actively trying to make me look bad?"

I started to laugh.

"No. But it works out well, doesn't it?" I challenged.

He rolled his eyes.

"You asking her?" George asked, his eyes trained in the same direction mine were. On Sway.

She was wearing her signature khaki pants and fitted green polo shirt that declared her 'Lumberjack Staff.' Though she'd changed her shoes.

They were white Converse that had the toes decorated with green rhinestones. The side of the shoe also had a green rhinestone number 49, which made me happy that she was wearing my number, even if it was understated.

It'd be better if she had that number tattooed on her cheek or something…

"Think she'll say yes?" he asked.

I nodded my head.

"Yep."

"So sure of yourself?" he asked.

I nodded again.

"Yep."

He snorted.

"Marriage is hard."

I turned my head to look at him.

"Yeah?"

He nodded.

"Yeah," he confirmed. "But it's worth it. I'd give my left nut to have my marriage back. Absolutely anything for just one more night with my arms wrapped around her."

Silence fell as the anthem started to play, and I closed my eyes and thanked God that Sway was mine.

That I would never—God willing—feel what Furious George was feeling at that moment.

***

Three hours and forty-one minutes later, I hit the game winning run straight over the right field wall.

The crowd around me went wild, and I started to run at a slow jog, stopping to slap hands with Sterling, the Shreveport Sparks in-fielder, as

I went.

"That was just lucky," Sterling called as I passed.

I raised a brow at him.

"Or maybe you're just unlucky," I countered.

He started to laugh, and his humor followed me as I made my way around the bases.

My eyes went to Gabe who was standing by the wall, a broad grin on his face as he looked down at his wife who was talking animatedly with her hands.

The moment I rounded home and started heading in their direction, I was pounced on, my teammates surrounding me as they congratulated me.

"Did you know that you passed up the lead in home runs this season with that hit?" someone yelled.

I turned to find a reporter directly behind my back, and I grinned.

"It feels damn good," I informed her. "Will you excuse me for a few seconds?"

I ducked and jived when the cooler of Powerade started heading for my head, and then cursed when I couldn't avoid the second cooler coming at me.

"Goddammit, you fuckers," I shouted as the red sports drink poured all over me, staining the white parts of my uniform instantly.

The boys chuckled as I flicked my hands out at my side, and I sighed as I made my way to Gabe.

Gabe was ready for me the moment I got there and passed me the velvet box without a word.

I took it and turned, heading back in the direction of Sway, who was standing at the top of the dugout steps watching me with a small smile on her face.

"That was a good game," she informed me once I was close enough to hear her over the roaring of the crowd, who were still there.

I grinned.

"Yep."

"You only got one home run, though," she teased. "I am a little bit disappointed."

I dropped down to one knee in front of her, and her eyes widened in alarm.

"What are you doing?" she asked shrilly.

I opened the box, and her eyes instantly filled with tears.

"Sway, will you marry me?"

Her mouth fell open, and then she threw herself at me.

Before I could react, we both fell backwards into the grass, and the crowd around us went wild.

"So, is that a yes?" I asked between her kisses.

She nodded and pushed up, using my stomach to steady herself, and I grunted as all the air left my body.

"Of course, it's a yes!" She started to giggle. "You're going to regret this, you know."

"How so?" I teased.

She leaned down so her face was only inches from mine.

"You're going to be on the front page of every single newspaper in the country," she promised.

I pushed her up so she was still straddling my legs, but I was upright, and lifted the velvet box from the grass where it'd fallen.

"I don't really care."

Then I slid that ring on her finger, where it would never, ever leave again.

I looked up into those beautiful blue eyes, now filled to overflowing with tears, and said the words she probably never thought she'd hear.

"You're the best superstition ever."

EPILOGUE

Forgiveness is divine. Telling someone to fuck off is even better.
-Note to self

Hancock

"I can't do it." She shook her head frantically. "I can't fucking do it."

"Come on. I'll go with you."

She shook her head faster.

"What's that?" I asked.

She turned her head to look in the direction I was pointing, and I chose that moment to push her over the edge.

The last look I got from her before she hit the water twenty feet below us was a look of betrayal and a promise for retribution.

I followed right behind her, of course, and swam towards her the moment I got my head about me.

"Don't talk to me, Hancock. I'm mad at you." She turned, viciously yanking down her goggles to cover her eyes. "I cannot believe you'd push the mother of your children off a cliff."

I chuckled as I swam up to her back, wrapping my arms around her belly as I kicked my feet to keep us both above water.

"I wouldn't have pushed you if you'd have jumped," I teased.

She sighed.

"I hate when you're right," she grumbled. "Now let's swim down there and look at these stupid fish you want to look at."

Then she disappeared into the clear depths, swimming toward the bottom as she turned her head left and right, taking in in the underwater scenery.

I tugged my goggles over my eyes, and fit the respirator in my mouth, and dove down, kicking my feet hard to get close to her.

My eyes stayed on her ass as I swam, and by the time I'd gotten to her, my cock was hard as a rock.

Which wasn't too surprising. She was in a freakin' bathing suit that left very little to the imagination.

She'd gained a little weight over our five-year marriage, but not enough to make a huge difference in her body.

She had stretch marks where before it was unblemished skin, and she had a little more of a pooch on her belly from our two kids growing inside of her, but other than that, she looked nearly identical to the day I met her.

And I could not find a single thing wrong with that.

Sway patted my arm, bringing my attention away from her ass, and to the fish that she was frantically pointing to.

I held my thumb up, and she widened her eyes behind the goggles.

The fish she was pointing at was a clownfish…the same fish that we saw on a daily basis back at our house thanks to our three-year-old little girl who was in love with all things *Nemo*.

She started to wiggle her arms as she shimmied in the water, and my eyes zeroed in straight for her breasts, the thin wisp of fabric that was barely containing them slipped, and her nipple popped out.

She immediately fixed it, but it was enough.

I had to have her.

Right then.

Reaching for her, I pulled her with me to a rock to steady us.

The moment my ass touched the large shelf, I pushed the waistband of my swim trunks down, exposing my erection.

Her eyes widened and she frantically started shaking her head, but I wouldn't take no for an answer.

I rarely ever did.

Not unless she really meant it.

But Sway liked to push the boundaries. She liked when I did things to her that she wouldn't do normally.

Right now being one of those times.

Pulling her towards me, I yanked her so her legs were on either side of my hips and moved her swimsuit bottoms to the side.

The moment my cock found the entrance to her pussy, I thrust inside, groaning into my respirator.

We'd never done this in water before. It was completely and utterly different than anything I'd ever felt before.

And the moment I came, a few minutes later, taking Sway with me, I knew it wouldn't be our last time. Even if we had to do this in our bathtub at home, it was getting done again.

It felt too good not to.

***

Five minutes later, she laughed breathlessly as we climbed our way out of the water.

"So, is that what we're going to do now that you're retired?" she teased, looking back over her shoulder at me.

"Of course," I teased, kicking my flippers off and bending down to pick them up. "What else is there to do?"

She snorted and headed for our towel, and I winced when I saw that someone had set up nearly directly next to us.

"Grab the blanket and move it over here," I indicated a tree that was casting some shade on a grassy area of the beach.

She picked up her phone, my phone and the keys and carefully shook out the blanket before walking it all over to the tree.

I threw my flippers on the ground next to the tree before taking the blanket from her and spreading it.

She dropped her stuff and headed back over to where we had our picnic basket and picked it up to bring it back over.

"What did you pack for us?" she asked.

I took out six Lunchables, and she started to laugh.

"What a great picnic, Hancock!" she snickered.

Without further ado, she grabbed one of the three pizza Lunchables, cheese only, and started building her lunch. Except she didn't eat them right. Something I'd learned over the course of five years of marriage to her.

She stacked them like a sandwich, and then ate all three at the same time.

It was weird, yes, but it was her. It was Sway. And I'd take Sway any way she came, because she was that important to me.

My eyes drifted to the water when a sudden movement caught my eye, and my eyes bulged when a man in his birthday suit started to walk to a blanket. The one that'd been right beside ours.

Spotting us, though, he veered off course and walked over, extending his hand to me.

I didn't take it.

Mainly because his cock was wiggling only inches away from Sway's face.

"Hi, my name is Frank," the man introduced himself.

After realizing I wasn't going to take his hand, he dropped it to his side.

That didn't make his smile go away, though.

Mine had, though.

"Do you mind, Frank, stepping away from my wife with your dick?" I snapped. "She's trying to eat, and she doesn't need your twig and berries waggling in her face while she does."

The man looked down at himself, then at Sway, before taking a large step back.

"My apologies," he said formally. "I didn't realize."

My ass.

He did realize.

You had to realize when your dick was that close to some other man's woman.

There was no way in hell he didn't know. None.

Appetite gone, I tossed my uneaten *Lunchables* back in the basket.

Sway did the same, and I knew then that she was in the same boat as me.

She was ready to go.

Now.

And I couldn't say I blamed her.

"Well it was nice meeting you, Frank," I lied as I stood up. "We'll see you around. We have a dolphin swimming experience to get to."

"Ohh, that sounds fun!" Frank said. "You'll have to let me know how you enjoyed it."

Yeah, right.

"Sure thing." I picked up my phone as well as Sway's and tossed them into the basket with our food. "See you around."

I hoped not.

"You too," Frank decreed with a wave.

Sway and I were around the rock that had secluded the little cove from the rest of the beach before I held up a hand and said, "Let me go over and tell the guy where to get his scuba gear back."

Sway nodded and waited while I handled it, slipping the guy a hundred-dollar bill since I knew what he was about to encounter.

"Did you tip him well?" Sway teased.

"A hundred bucks."

"It's not enough," she shivered in revulsion. "Did you see the size of his dick? I didn't know they came that big!"

I slapped her ass.

"You're not supposed to notice anybody's dick but mine," I informed her.

She snorted. "Yes, Master."

My eyes flared.

"You can call me that later in bed, okay?"

She sighed. "You're so predictable."

***

"Are you going to call me master?" I asked, gathering Sway's hair in my fist as I urged her faster.

She threw her head back, but not before she said what she had to say.

"Why would I call you master when I'm the one doing all the work?" she asked. "Maybe *you* should be calling *me* master."

She giggled at the look on my face, and I lifted my hips, meeting her thrust as she came down on top of my dick, causing her to gasp.

"Jesus Christ," she whispered frantically. "I'm coming."

I waited until I knew she was finished to unload my release inside of her, and she nearly came a second time if the rippling in her pussy was anything to go by.

She panted as she leaned forward, resting her head just below my chin.

Her hand lifted to stroke my beard, and I sighed as our hearts slowed.

"Are you going to get rid of this now that you are done playing?" she asked, stroking me.

I loved my beard.

Loved how it made Sway's skin redden when I was touching her with it. Loved how she stared at me, stroking it like she was doing now. Most of all, though, I loved that she loved it.

If she hated it, then I'd get rid of it.

But Sway wouldn't ever ask, and to be honest, I was sure she liked it more than I did.

But before I could answer her question, a clapping filled the air.

"Crikey, mate," someone said, interrupting my post-orgasm bliss. "I need a cigarette after that. Good on you, bloke!"

Sway stiffened and she immediately stood, my dick falling to my bare thigh as she rushed into the room.

I followed her, coming to a stop in the bathroom doorway as she paced back and forth while waiting for the shower to warm.

"What's wrong?" I teased.

She tossed me a glare.

"I'm fat, and some guy just watched my fat jiggle while I rode you," she said point blank.

My brows rose.

"You might have a few extra pounds now, but I love every new thing about you. Every extra inch. Every extra stretch mark. Every extra dimple. Every extra pound." I started to run my lips down the length of her neck. "I just love *you*. Who the fuck cares about what anyone else thinks?"

She sighed, but her head was lifted, and her eyes were shining.

"You know," she said, walking towards me. "You're a really great man."

I grinned.

"I know."

"And you're so humble."

I winked.

"Hard working."

She lifted her hand to my beard once again.

"A good daddy."

My heart swelled.

"But most of all, you're the best husband a woman could ask for."

Her mouth came to my cheek, my beard hair rubbing coarsely against her baby soft skin.

Then, she ruined it all by opening her mouth. Closing her lips around my beard hair, and then pulling.

"Why do you insist on *Billy Goating* me?"

She burst out laughing.

"'Cause I like the reaction I get out of you when I do it."

I pulled her to me when she turned to step into the shower, wrapping both of my thick arms around her chest and middle.

"You forgot to say you love me," I informed her.

She looked at me over her shoulder.

"Maybe. But I'll show you if you join me in the shower."

"Promise?" I asked.

She smiled. "Promise."

ABOUT THE AUTHOR

Lani Lynn Vale is married to the love of her life that she met in high school. She fell in love with him because he was wearing baseball pants. Ten years later they have three perfectly crazy children and a cat named Demon who likes to wake her up at ungodly times in the night. They live in the greatest state in the world, Texas. She writes contemporary and romantic suspense, and has a love for all things romance. You can find Lani in front of her computer writing away in her fictional characters' world...that is until her husband and kids demand sustenance in the form of food and drink.

Printed in Dunstable, United Kingdom